Date Due

D1266750

JL   APR 2 '96

SLOW FUSE

MASAKO TOGAWA

Translated from the Japanese by Simon Prentis

SLOW FUSE

Pantheon Books   New York

Library of Congress Cataloging-in-Publication Data

Togawa, Masako, 1933–
[Fukai shissoku. English]
Slow fuse / Masako Togawa;
translated from the Japanese by Simon Prentis.
p. cm.
ISBN 0-679-41862-8
I. Title.
PL862.03F813   1995
895.6'35—dc20
95-11771
CIP

Book design by M. Kristen Bearse

Manufactured in the United States of America

First American Edition

2 4 6 8 9 7 5 3 1

To Mr. J.

Contents

SLOW FUSE

The Woman in the White Room

One

Behind a line of withered cypress trees at the entrance to the apartment house, I could see the blue water of a swimming pool. The water in the pool looked as if it hadn't been changed for about six months, and was obviously going stagnant. Several weather-beaten deck chairs and torn umbrellas lay abandoned at the pool's edge, a reminder that summer was long gone.

I stopped in front of the bulletin board at the side of the narrow path leading to the pool. It was placed so that visitors to the apartments could not help noticing that a swimming pool was there, whether they liked it or not. The sign said something to the effect that the pool was for members only, and that no one else was allowed to use it. Presumably only residents could become members.

The white sign stood solid and foursquare, as if proud of its role as a notice which forbade things. "No

fishing. No diving. No peeping. No shouting," it announced. All the forbidden words I knew would excite
my patient suddenly flashed through my mind. He too
had probably seen this board before anything else. For
a few moments I thought about the effect it might have
had on him, but there was nothing that immediately
came to mind.

Moving away from the pool, I waited somewhat im-
patiently at the entrance to the apartment house while
the automatic doors slowly opened. During these few
moments I noticed that the uniformed concierge at the
reception desk was observing me carefully. He probably always watched people coming into the building in
the same way. In fact, it was quite certain that he would
have seen my patient. The question was, how clear an
image of him would remain in a memory that would
now be some weeks old?

"Would you please call Mrs. Owada on the sixth
floor, and tell her that Dr. Uemura has arrived," I said
to the concierge. I simply gave him my name, without
mentioning the hospital. There was no need for that, I
felt.

The concierge pressed the switch on the intercom
and announced my arrival. A woman's voice, somewhat
indistinct through the speaker, answered the clear tones
of the doorman standing in front of me. It was a
strangely metallic voice, without any trace of emotion.
It would be impossible to guess her age from her voice
alone. In any case, it was very unlikely that hearing it
would arouse any particular desire. It was completely
different from the seductive tones used almost uncon-

sciously by female announcers in department stores and theaters.

Wondering what lay behind the dryness of the woman's abrupt "Please send him up," I walked over to the elevator. The glint of professional concern that had shone in the concierge's eyes when I entered the building had now faded. He seemed to have no awareness of my business there.

The Owadas' apartment was right at the end of a long corridor leading from the elevator. The center of the building was constructed as a triangular skylight for the staircase, and its blue glass made it seem like a botanical garden or an aquarium. When I pressed the bell, the metallic voice sounded again from the intercom at the side of the door. It was as dry and lifeless as before.

"Who's that?" said the voice.

"It's Dr. Uemura. I've just come up from the lobby," I said.

"Just a moment, please." The door opened about two inches, and half an eye looked out. The door was still held with a very robust-looking chain.

"I called earlier from the hospital. I believe your husband is aware that I am coming," I said, taking out a card and holding it through the gap, with the chain still attached to the door. The woman took it with her thin fingers. After examining my card thoroughly, she finally took the chain off the door.

"I'm sorry. I've become rather nervous of late," she said.

"I quite understand. Please don't concern yourself

about it," I said, in my best bedside manner. I still wasn't quite sure how I should present myself to her, or what words I should use.

The woman led me through to a sitting room that doubled as a very bright sunroom. There was a long-stemmed rubber plant with shiny oval leaves, and some white French furniture arranged rather prettily beside it. A tightly woven lace tablecloth and a white sheep-skin rug completed the overall impression of white-ness. I immediately sensed the subconscious desire on the part of the person living here. It was most likely a wish for purity, I thought.

"It's a nice room, isn't it," I said.

"Thank you. It certainly gets the sun, anyway."

I walked over to the window. Beyond the double glazing, I could see the deep blue of the pool I had no-ticed earlier. The sun was casting shadows on the water, and the wind was chasing ripples across its surface.

"I understand that you wanted to come and ask about a patient of yours. What exactly do you wish to know?" asked the woman.

Without waiting for an answer, she sat down on a white chair. She was wearing a loose-knit red sweater which was quite obviously intended for wearing around the house, but her tight black skirt showed off a pair of well-formed, rounded knees and rather muscular long straight legs. She was wearing sheer nylon tights of a much darker color than her skin, and sure to catch the eye of any man. It seemed strangely out of balance with the rather sporty sweater and the kangaroo-skin slippers she was wearing, which gave a distinctly casual impression. Almost without thinking, I began to compare the description in my patient's statement with the woman who was sitting in front of me. I knew that he had been obsessively drawn to the woman's legs. But that would be something that any man would feel, myself included.

"I would like you to understand that what I'm about to tell you is a confidential matter, which I am party to in my capacity as a doctor," I began, somewhat hesitantly.

I was conscious that my voice was still rather stilted. I tried to remember the soft, soothing tones that I used in talking to my patients, but somehow I couldn't manage it. Perhaps it was because it takes a certain amount of courage for a doctor to ask a woman, and especially a beautiful woman whom he is meeting for the first time, whether or not she has been raped.

"It's about something that happened four months ago, on the twentieth of December last year," I said, removing some documents from my leather briefcase and leaning over them, trying to broach the subject without allowing my emotions to surface.

Two

"So, what exactly is all this about?" she asked. Her neat hands, resting on her knees, stiffened almost imperceptibly.

"Well, to start at the beginning, I should explain that

a week ago the police took into custody a student who
had tried to commit suicide," I said. "He was threatening to throw himself off the roof of a department
store. It was reported briefly in the papers. Perhaps you
saw the article?"

"No."

"The student's name is Akio Tanno, and he is
twenty years old. Since his moods fluctuate between violent aggression and complete suppression of his feelings, the police asked us to look after him and place
him under observation. It fell to me to interview this
young man."

The woman shifted her gaze to my card, which was
lying on the table. It gave my name, the university hospital where I worked, and the telephone number of the
psychiatric unit I was attached to.

"When you say 'interview,' do you mean psychoanalysis?" she asked.

"Yes, we tried as best we could to establish the motive for the attempted suicide. We gave him electric
shock therapy followed by three short interviews, each
lasting about an hour. During the third interview he
began to tell us a very strange tale."

I slowly flicked through my documents. The woman
continued to show absolutely no reaction.

"According to his story, Akio Tanno worked as a delivery boy for holiday gifts at a department store in
Ginza from the fifth to the twentieth of December. It
seems he wanted to earn some money to pay for a ski
trip. On the twentieth he was sent to deliver a bottle of
whiskey to an apartment in Leila Mansions. Some time

after two in the afternoon, he had the concierge at the reception desk announce his arrival, and made his way up to apartment 601 on the sixth floor. When he got there, he went inside briefly to hand over the whiskey and get it signed for. Up to that point, everything was just like any normal delivery. Being a somewhat shy person, he did not look directly at the customer's face, except for a brief moment when handing over the whiskey. Nonetheless he was left with the impression of a strikingly beautiful woman. The lady in apartment 601 had made up her face carefully, and looked as though she was just about to go out."

I was summarizing the boy's statement, and at that point I looked up and shifted my attention to the woman sitting before me. The shape of her lips was emphasized by the use of a slightly orange lipstick, and her light gray eyeshadow highlighted a pair of almond-shaped eyes of the kind popular in Europe.

"I always do my makeup in the morning when I wake up, even when my husband is away. I don't want to just let myself go simply because I'm at home," she said.

"Yes, I quite understand." As I replied, I let my gaze run momentarily over her shapely, attractive legs with their tightly held knees, before returning to my documents.

"As he asked her to sign for the delivery he noticed that her hands were wet. The following conversation then ensued between the two of them: 'I'm sorry, there's something wrong with the tap and I can't turn it off, you know.' 'The washer must be loose, then, I suppose. I know a little bit about plumbing. I used to do it as a student job.' 'Oh, you're a student, are you?' 'Yes, that's right, at the university.' 'I see, well that's convenient. I wonder if you could have a look at the tap for me?' 'Well, I don't mind trying, if you'd like me to.' So Akio Tanno went in through to the kitchen of apartment 601 and fixed the tap for her. That was on the twentieth of December. Nothing unusual occurred on that occasion. The woman brought tea and cookies for him, and he ate them before leaving. Is this story correct?"

"Yes, that's absolutely right." The woman's voice seemed to be desperately suppressing some emotion. I remembered the lifeless metallic voice that came from the intercom by the side of the door. I had the strange feeling that it could hardly be possible that these two voices belonged to the same person.

"The second time he visited apartment 601 was two weeks later," I continued. "But on that occasion the woman did not allow him up. Unlike before, he felt he was being coldly turned away."

"He asked me how the tap was, and I simply said that I had had no more trouble with it." Her reply was brusque.

"If you had only let him up you might not have hurt his feelings," I said.

"But I hadn't put on my makeup, and I wasn't ready to meet anyone," she said, defensively.

"I wonder if you'd mind if I asked you to read the next part of his statement yourself," I said.

"Yes, I would. Please continue reading it yourself." She had reverted to her expressionless voice. I returned my gaze to Akio Tanno's densely written statement. My plan had been to make her read it herself so that I could observe her reactions, but I had been foiled.

I lit a cigarette. My previous feeling that it would be difficult for me to keep on reading the statement had now gone completely. Her cold reaction had brought out something sadistic in me. Letting the ash from my cigarette drop onto the documents, I slowly continued reading.

" 'I (Akio Tanno) am determined to see that woman once again whatever happens. The more I think about it, the more obsessive my fantasies become. I want to rip off the clothes that cover her slim, slender body . . .' "

She suddenly interrupted me. "That's enough. I'll read it myself."

"If you wouldn't mind."

The woman took the statement from me and began reading, and I saw a slight flushing round her eyes, as if in anger. I also noticed a sudden nervous spasm, which passed over her beautiful left cheek like a dark shadow. It was quite clearly the beginning of an attack of hysteria.

She was no longer reading the report. Her eyes were merely playing over the words. I had no choice but to take up Akio Tanno's story again.

"The third time he visited this apartment he brought with him a delivery box, which he had covered in the wrapping paper of the department store. It was quite a large box, about four foot six by eighteen inches. But of course there was no delivery, and he had something else hidden inside."

"Why on earth would he do a thing like that?" The woman suddenly looked up and stared at my face quizzically. Her eyes were blazing with suppressed anger.

"It was to make the person in the apartment open the door. He first went to the lobby and got the concierge to say that there was a delivery from the department store. Unlike the second time, when he was turned away, he was able to pass quite easily through the reception area and make his way up to the door of the apartment. When she heard that it was a delivery from the department store, the woman opened the door. However, she was suspicious, and didn't remove the chain from the door. That was precisely why he had brought the large box with him."

"That was very clever of him, wasn't it?" she said.

"Well, it certainly shows how determined he was. He attempted to put the box through the gap in the door with the chain still attached, but the box was about two inches too big and would not go in. The woman closed the door and removed the chain. So now he'd finally succeeded in getting into the apartment."

"What on earth was in the box, I wonder?" She looked at me with a deadpan expression.

"In his statement he merely says a long weapon. He absolutely refuses to say any more. We interviewed him on this point for nearly thirty minutes. We used free association based on a method developed in America by a professor at U.C.L.A., which is in effect a form of forced confession. It's a method where you keep on asking question after question on the same point, and slowly gather details about whatever it is that the person is trying to hide. Using this method, we are eighty percent certain that this weapon was either a shotgun or a hunting rifle."

"You mean he handed over a box containing a shotgun to the other person?" Her question seemed intentionally different from what my patient had said in his statement. It was as if she wanted me to understand that she hadn't read through to the end of it. Unless . . . I pretended not to hear what she had said, in the same way that one ignores the initial resistance of a patient in an interview.

"He'd carried out his plan exactly as he had hoped. He then told her that just a few moments before, he had carelessly dropped the box, and it was his responsibility as a delivery boy to check the contents of the package, to see that nothing had been broken. He removed the wrapping paper himself, and opening the lid of the box, took out the gun and pointed it at her. He already had a murderous glint in his eyes. 'Don't scream! If you scream I'll really shoot you!' he shouted out, almost gasping. Convinced that he was quite serious, the woman gave up the idea of resisting and did exactly what he told her. He told her to lock the door, put the chain on, and take the phone off the hook. He then used the gun to break the wire connecting the intercom with the reception desk downstairs. She begged him not to be violent with her because her husband would soon be returning. She even said that if he let her go then and there, she wouldn't tell the police and would keep quiet about the whole thing. He seemed to flinch slightly at that, but then shook his head. 'I've checked up on your husband, you know. I know that he's a pilot with an airline, and at this very moment is due to be flying into London.' Being the person he is, he had prepared for his actions almost too minutely. Once the wheels of a tragedy begin to roll, they develop a momentum of their own that's somehow independent of the people involved, even if they decide they want to stop. When the woman realized that he knew where her husband was, she lost all further will to resist. She seemed to fall into a state of terror at the thought that she was about to be involved in something horrifying, and couldn't bring herself to answer anything he said. She just stood there blankly, like a lifeless doll."

"How terrible for her, if such a thing had really happened." The woman turned her gaze away from me and looked out the window. She appeared to be looking at something floating on the surface of the pool. It looked as if it was a kind of duckweed. There was a sudden shift in the sunlight that filled the room, so that now it just touched the upper part of the rubber plant.

"However, what happened next was completely different from what he had expected." I leaned over the statement again and read it quite slowly, as if Akio Tanno himself were reading it.

" 'It was about then that I began to feel a burning sensation inside my head, bursting to get out. I started dripping with sweat, until it ran down into my eyes. I had no intention of touching the woman; I was just glad that I could see her in front of me. As long as I could see her, I was sure I would be able to build an image of her in my mind. At first I felt ashamed of what I was doing. But then this sensation suddenly turned into a feeling of ecstasy. I'd been looking at her so long that she'd become fixed in my mind, almost like a sculpture. I was suddenly overcome with the feeling that I wanted to destroy the real woman who was standing in front of me. As if driven on by this feeling, I pulled the trigger, and felt a powerful recoil in my arms. The white, naked woman's body collapsed as if it were crumbling away. I thought to myself that I had finally killed someone. The world around me was destroyed by that gunshot. But then I came to my senses, threw away the gun I was holding, and ran out down the fire escape."

The woman suddenly stood up with a hysterical laugh, and I stopped reading the statement.

"But if that were really true, how is it that I am still alive?" she said.

"Well, that's precisely why we decided not to give this statement to the police. We feel that this story is merely a product of our patient's persecution complex. We think he invented this murder story because he wants to punish himself."

The woman was silent.

Three

The sun was setting in the west. The woman was standing by the window in the last rays of the sun, her back turned to me. A long shadow stretched away from her feet. I was suddenly struck by the thought that there was a very lithe and supple body beneath her red sweater. Had Akio Tanno really threatened her with a gun and forced her to have sex with him? I began to have an inkling of just how frightening an experience that would have been.

"His guilt feelings are too strong. If we can establish the truth of what happened here, he will begin to be able to return to normality. But if we leave things as they are, he will continue to use the murder story to avoid facing his sexual feelings, which are what he is really afraid of, and bury them deep in his subconscious."

"Are you asking me to give evidence that he raped me?" she asked.

"Even if any proceedings simply take the form of an out-of-court settlement, I'd like to ask you to file a formal report on the incident with the police. The police will of course maintain absolute confidentiality in the matter. The only way that we can help this boy is to have him punished under the law. I'm sorry to cause you more trouble than you have already been through, but the fact is that if we make no attempt to resolve the matter, he will certainly make another attempt to kill himself. As a doctor I fully understand the uncomfortable position that you find yourself in, but I'm afraid I must ask you to help."

She turned very slowly to look at me. It was as if she had given very careful and deliberate thought to the whole affair. As the room was in shadow, I could not see the expression on her face.

"How old are you?" she asked.

"Twenty-seven." I answered her question without understanding what she meant by it. She looked at me with a sorrowful stare. I felt that she was pitying my ignorance of the world.

"I see. Well, I understand perfectly well what you are saying, but I really cannot say that something happened when it did not. It's true that the boy did come a second time, but there was certainly no third visit, nor a box from the department store, nor any such thing. I'm sure that it is all just a figment of his imagination."

She walked toward me, allowing me to clearly see the slight smile playing on her lips. Without her saying so directly, there was no doubt that she was asking me to leave. The tension that had built up within me was now released. Had all the conversations I had had with my patient really been so pointless and absurd?

Saying that I might come back to ask her help again if I had any more information from my patient, I reluctantly rose to take my leave. The woman walked me to the door, saying with a smile that I should feel free to call on her again. Using the shoehorn she offered me, I bent down to put on my shoes. From that position I could see a small scrap of wrapping paper poking out from under the doormat. It appeared to have the name of the department store written on it. Resisting the temptation to pick it up, I stood up and made my way out into the corridor. From behind me I heard the sound of the lock, and the chain being attached to the door.

Leaving the building by the path at the side of the pool, I glanced once again at the sign with its members-only regulations, before looking up the side of the building past the smart brick-faced verandas to see if I could identify the Owadas' apartment. It was at that point that I finally remembered that Mrs. Owada's first name was Hisako. When I'd been in the building, the only thing that had come to mind was the word "woman," which Akio Tanno had constantly used to refer to her in his statement.

I walked down the gentle slope past the ivy-covered wall that ran alongside the building, and found a telephone in front of the pharmacy. I called the hospital to find out how my patient was. When I got through to the nurse, her voice sounded tense and nervous.

"Doctor, your patient in room seven, Akio Tanno, has been missing from his bed for the last hour. We think he's probably run away. Please come back as soon as you can. . . ."

Interplay in Black and White

One

The airport was almost deserted. The only people in sight were a young couple admiring the new car on display on a trade stand decorated with bunches of plastic roses, and a middle-aged man slumped on a bench in front of a television which was droning out the evening news. Most of the last flights due in from Europe, the southern routes via Hong Kong and the polar routes via Anchorage, had already arrived.

The arrivals lounge was also empty, as most passengers and their luggage had now passed through customs and disappeared with the friends and relatives who had come to meet them. The only people still left were airline staff and those, including myself, who had come to meet passengers off the last flight of the day and were simply killing time.

I made my way up onto the floor above the lobby, and went into one of the bars there that were already

starting to close for the night. Most of these bars, normally full with people meeting their friends, already
had their stools piled up on the tables like a classroom
at the end of the day. I sat down at the circular counter,
and with a brief sigh, ordered a soda water. I really felt
like a beer, but I was worried that even a small drink
might shake my concentration. After all, I had to keep
my wits about me even more than I would when inter-
viewing a patient.

The girl behind the counter, her long blue apron
edged in red, put the colorless glass of soda water down
in front of me with a smile. It was clear from her look
that she was interested in me. Either that or she was
really enjoying herself for some reason. On the far side
of the counter there was another, rather thin girl working. She was wearing the same smart apron that the
other girl had on, but had dark bags under her eyes
that no amount of makeup could hide. She seemed
to be in a bad mood, and clumsily placed a plate of
soup in front of a rather fat, foreign-looking gentleman seated at the counter. She was clearly overtired
and frustrated. My thoughts moved on to the job at
hand.

*You see how simple it is? People give themselves away
with every movement they make. The best thing is not to
worry about meeting him. You're sure to pick up something
useful that way.*

I was trying to reassure myself, but my doubts were
not so easily shaken. *You can only see through people
when they don't know you're watching. If they're prepared for you, or set out to trick you from the start, it's*

easy to be fooled or draw the wrong conclusion. My conscience was playing devil's advocate.

Just then, I heard the soft tones of a flight announcement. "Flight HBY 806 from Hong Kong, due in at 22.30, will be arriving shortly at gate 13." I glanced down at my watch: it was nearly eleven o'clock. We had arranged to meet here at ten forty-five.

From the far end of the airport I could hear the roar of an approaching jet. A DC-8 with its red landing lights on was making its final approach. Hisako Owada's husband would be at the controls of Flight 806. As he prepared for landing, the most stressful moment of a flight, his problems with his wife would probably be far from his mind. And so, no doubt, would be the appointment that he had with me, the psychiatrist.

I was just lighting my second cigarette when Captain Owada walked into the bar in his smart flight-officer's uniform. He was carrying a black briefcase, and had with him a young flight attendant. She looked about twenty-five years old, and as they approached she glanced at Captain Owada and said something to him quickly. The look in her eyes was bright and exuberant. For a moment, it almost seemed like a flicker of passion. Captain Owada kept his composure and continued to look straight ahead toward where I was sitting at the bar. The expression on his face was like that of a pilot looking for visual landmarks when landing. I waved my hand briefly. Given what we had to discuss, I wanted to keep the formalities to a minimum.

"I'm sorry to be late, but we were delayed at Hong Kong with some maintenance problems," he said apologetically.

He sat down next to me and ordered a whiskey and water. He spoke with a calm and reassuring voice, giving the impression of a man who thought everything through carefully before speaking.

The flight attendant who was with him nodded briefly in my direction before going to sit at a window seat some distance away. Looking a little closer at her, I could see she was a pretty girl with a dark complexion, almost Indonesian. Despite being somewhat plump, she had a shapely pair of legs and probably had no difficulty attracting men.

"How's the weather in Rome?" I asked. I decided to start by asking him an innocuous question, unrelated to my real point of interest. Although the weather was hardly an ideal topic, it was better than nothing.

"It's rather rainy at this time of year," he answered, after a brief pause. I watched him raise his glass to his mouth. He had taut, masculine lips, suggesting a strong will that was obviously well able to hold desires and emotions in check.

"I wonder if you were able to meet my wife?" he asked. He said this in a rather worried tone, as if unsettled by the fact that I hadn't mentioned it. His choice of words was formal, showing that he was conscious of speaking to a doctor.

"Yes, indeed I was," I said. "As we agreed, I visited her at your apartment this afternoon."

"I see." He looked down at the amber liquid in his

glass. I had absolutely no idea what might be going through his mind.

"Your wife did not accept the last part of my patient's statement," I said.

"And what do you suppose that means?" He turned to face me more directly.

"She told me that the student had come twice about the tap, but insisted that the third visit he mentions in his statement did not take place. She also quite categorically denied that the student had brought with him a box large enough to contain a shotgun, or that there had been any violence."

He made no reply to this, but instead turned back toward his glass again.

Two

"What do you make of what my wife told you, Doctor? Do you take it at face value?" He asked me this in rather a low voice, after a considerable pause. He was clearly unable to make up his mind about it. I waited a moment before replying. Was it better to avoid hurting a person's feelings, or to face up to the truth even if it meant opening up old wounds?

My visit to the white room in Mrs. Owada's apartment that afternoon had in fact been made at his request. It is one of the first rules of medicine that a doctor should always consider the feelings of all parties concerned when treating a patient. After all, in normal circumstances it's hardly possible, even for a doctor, to go to a married woman's apartment and ask her whether or not she has been raped. But it's different if the husband specifically requests it. In that case it can be part of the treatment.

Akio Tanno had mailed a copy of his statement to Mrs. Owada's husband. If he was not going to be punished by the police, he probably thought that it was quite natural that he should tell the other person who had a right to punish him—the husband of the woman he had raped.

"I killed your wife with a long weapon hidden in a box wrapped in department store paper." That was the gist of what he had said. I suddenly remembered that Captain Owada had never shown me this letter which he claimed my patient had sent. Instead of replying to his question, I decided to ask him about that.

"Would you mind showing me the letter my patient sent you?" I asked.

He opened up the black leather briefcase sitting on his knees, fished out a crumpled envelope from among a jumble of flight schedules, notebooks, and English paperbacks, and handed it to me. Was the battered state of the envelope a sign of Akio Tanno's violence, or of the agonizing Captain Owada had gone through, unable to make up his mind whether to tear it up or to confront his wife with it? In the end, perhaps he had felt that the easiest course was to take the letter to the psychiatric unit mentioned in the letter.

"When I told you about it before on the phone, I

couldn't show it to you because I had left it in Rome,"
he said, with a blank expression in his eyes.

"Do you have somewhere in Rome where you can
leave your personal papers, then?" I asked.

"Yes, although the airline staff usually stay at a hotel
provided by the airline, I have a room which I rent
from a friend."

"Does your wife know about this room?"

"No, she doesn't, although I suspect she may. . . she
may guess it exists." I felt that he'd been on the point
of saying "she may have found out about it," but
had changed his mind. No doubt he had thought
that would've been too definite. Captain Owada and
I had agreed right from the beginning that he
would speak honestly to me about his relations with his
wife.

Honestly, openly, and without hiding anything.
These were the usual requests made by a psychiatrist to
a patient. Of course the patient initially resisted this,
but in the end they always opened up. At the very least,
with the help of an analyst they usually made an effort
to untie some of the threads binding the deeper parts
of their mind. However, healthy people were different.
They had a built-in defense mechanism which led
them to protect their secrets at all costs, and if this
came into play I could be led quite unwittingly down
the wrong path.

I looked directly at him. He, for his part, was acting
as if he were my patient, albeit slightly mischievously.
But it didn't fool me. On the contrary, I was beginning
to have my doubts. When I looked carefully at it, the

letter that he said Akio Tanno had sent him had the name of an Italian manufacturer printed in very small letters on the bottom.

Could it perhaps be that the letter supposedly sent by my patient had in fact been written by Captain Owada? But what possible motive could he have had for doing such a thing? I spread out the wrinkled paper once again, and tried to memorize what it said. I wanted to think this over very carefully. The writing on the paper curved around on itself as if it had been written by a left-handed person.

"I write this in haste to you as the husband, to inform you that your dearly beloved wife has been killed. She was killed with a long weapon. Please return this long weapon, which was hidden inside a box. The person who killed your wife is Akio Tanno, a student currently admitted to the psychiatric unit at the National University Hospital. Please notify the above for further details."

In part, the writing was quite clearly characteristic of the confusion typical of schizophrenics. That said, however, this degree of disorder could easily be imitated by anyone with a mind to do so. The final sentence, "please notify the above for further details," should quite obviously have been "please contact the above for further details" or "please refer to the above for further details." It could even be said that the use of the word "notify" showed the pain in the writer's mind, a pain which he had clearly felt while waiting vainly for some notification. But if that were the case, what was it that the writer had waited so long to be notified about? The results of university entrance exams would be a definite possibility.

"Perhaps we should move on, Doctor. It seems they're about to close the bar here," Captain Owada said, rising to go.

"In that case, then, let's arrange to meet another day," I suggested. "You must be tired now, and if you wouldn't mind coming to see me at the hospital, I could make time to talk to you any time."

He watched me replacing the letter in the envelope, and then opened his mouth as if he had just remembered something. Perhaps it was the thing that he had most wanted to ask.

"What do you think, Doctor, on the basis of your visit to my wife? Do you think it may be possible that she was raped? Of course my wife denies it, but I feel sure myself that the phrase 'killed with a long weapon' in the letter suggests some sort of sexual relationship. . . ."

The expression on his face as he spoke was that of a clever student who has been asked a question he hasn't prepared for. He spoke with composure, but it was an unconfident and awkward statement.

"Unfortunately, psychoanalysis isn't such a simple matter," I said. "It's easy for an amateur to make mistakes by applying the obvious formula. For the present I believe we should take your wife's word as it stands." I tried my best to maintain the tone of a professional counselor.

He looked to me as if he was about forty. He was much older than me, but that did not change the fact that I was a doctor. I remembered the words of a professor at a short course I had attended once at the University of Chicago, who said that rather than being more sophisticated, psychiatrists should strive to be more humane. As we rose to leave, I caught sight of the profile of the flight attendant sitting by the window, just as she brought a spoon filled with ice cream to her shapely lips.

"I realize that this may be very difficult to arrange, but I would be most grateful if you would allow me the opportunity to meet your patient," Captain Owada said in a very polite and subdued manner as he signed the bill for our drinks.

"I'm sorry I have to tell you this," I said, "but my patient escaped from the ward while I was visiting your wife this afternoon."

"But wasn't he being kept under observation?" he asked.

"Yes, he was, but my staff are not the police. Of course it still remains our responsibility."

His face suddenly looked much older. "Well, if you'll excuse me, I have some business to attend to in my office," he said.

As we reached the lobby, he extended a hand to me, as is the fashion abroad. The four gold bands on his captain's uniform shone like the trim on a car.

I walked over to the television in the lobby area and lit a cigarette. After about five minutes, the flight attendant who had been with him emerged from the bar, but she pretended not to notice me and walked straight to the airline office. The thought of her firm young body hidden within the dark green of her uniform inflamed a violent passion within me. It was the same sharp jolt of desire I had felt one day in a hot, humid airport in the Middle East. As I sat sweltering beneath a slowly turning fan, I couldn't take my eyes off a young girl squatting beside me, almost naked but for a sari . . .

When I made my way down from the lobby to the arrivals lounge, the screen with the flight arrivals information still showed that flight HBY 806 was expected at 22.30.

Three

When I got back to the hospital, I found that not only the doctor on duty but also the head of the psychiatric unit and the hospital director were in an emergency meeting which had been going on since the early evening.

It wasn't difficult to see how the escape of a patient would have upset the hospital director. The head of the unit would probably be doing his best to calm him down, to reassure him that the patient would be found in a few days.

"You're very late, Doctor. Where have you been?" asked head nurse Motoko Kusano. She came bustling into my room just as I got back, almost as if she'd been chasing me. She was only twenty-five years old, but was very good at her job, and her motherly touch never failed to win a smile and relax both staff and patients.

There was also a side to her welcoming grin that at times seemed to have a distinctly sexual edge.

"I've just been to see Captain Owada, the husband of the woman Akio Tanno talks about in his statement," I said.

"You've been working hard," she said.

"With an escaped patient on our hands, I thought I should try to find out as much as I could. We need to get all the information we can, whatever the source."

"Yes, Doctor, you're quite right . . . and that reminds me, I should tell you that the director has given us just three days. He has agreed to keep it quiet for the time being, but if we can't find him after that, they'll have to tell the police, and the head of the unit will have to take full responsibility. The director was absolutely furious that we let him escape. He said that considering that the police had entrusted him to our care, we hadn't taken the necessary precautions. You could hear his voice outside in the corridor. He's one of the old school, you know. He wouldn't really rest easy unless we had iron bars on all the windows . . ."

"Well, I suppose he's entitled to his point of view. But it would've helped if he'd given us a week," I said.

"We only got three days because the head of the unit persuaded him, you know. At the beginning he was saying he would only give us twenty-four hours." It sounded as if she was sympathizing with me. But the fact was that direct responsibility for looking after the patient lay with her and her nurses.

"What was he wearing when he escaped?" I asked. I had forgotten to ask this earlier.

"We found a rolled-up pair of pajamas thrown away in one of the stalls of the hospital toilet. And a pair of green overalls that were in the stall have turned up missing. It seems he probably put them on before escaping," she said.

I had known from the beginning of the whole affair that my patient meticulously planned everything he did. He must have planned this escape with careful forethought as well. He was definitely not the sort of patient who just impulsively makes a run for it.

I got up and walked over to the window. From my room I could see the incinerator at the back of the hospital, and the cobbled path running to the toilet. Akio Tanno's room was in the same building as the psychiatric unit. He would have been able to see the incinerator and the overalls used by the workmen. He must have seen all this from his bed and planned his escape. I began to get a sense of the detailed planning of this young man, and to feel a certain admiration for him.

As I did so, the thought crossed my mind that his statement might just be the truth after all. The idea of using a large delivery box as an excuse to get past a door held securely by lock and chain seemed much too practical to be simply fantasy. But then again, if he had actually done what he said in the statement, it meant that he really had killed someone with that long weapon. I felt a sudden chill go through me.

"Doctor . . . ," Motoko Kusano was calling me, this time in her formal head nurse's voice. While I knew it was part of a nurse's training not to show your emotion while working, I sensed that this artificial tone was an attempt to hide her true feelings.

"Are you angry with us about the escape?" she asked.

"No, not at all. I'm sure you all did your best," I said.

"I don't know if it was our best. . . ." Her voice gradually trailed away. I could tell from her behavior that there was something else behind Akio Tanno's escape.

"Is there something you want to tell me?" I asked.

"As a matter of fact, yes, there is," she said. "When we were keeping an eye on him in his bed, the nurse on duty asked me if I would take over to let her get away for a while." The on-duty nurse was a rather large, silent woman in her forties.

"And what has that got to do with it?" I asked.

"She said that she wanted to attend her son's graduation, so I swapped shifts with her."

"I don't have any objection to that," I said. I was fairly liberal about these things. I didn't feel there was any need to stick to a rigid timetable about work.

"But you see . . ." She couldn't bring herself to go on. I had an inkling of what the problem was.

"Did he . . . did he make advances to you?" I asked. It was the rule that male nurses should attend all difficult patients, and even where there was no fear of violence, that an older and more experienced nurse should always be on hand. This was done mainly to avoid working a patient up unnecessarily. However, due to staff shortages, there were occasions where young and inexperienced nurses had to be used to monitor patients.

"But you have quite enough experience, and the patient could hardly be said to be seriously ill," I said.

"Please don't make excuses for me," she said. "It was quite obviously my fault. You see, I had just put my lipstick on. I was just about to go home when the other nurse suddenly came and asked me to substitute for her. . . ." She said this in a voice trembling with emotion, but having managed to get the words out, she immediately reverted to her professional voice as she explained what happened next.

"I was sitting by the window reading a book. After a while I felt he was staring at me in a strange way. When I turned to try to reassure him, I noticed that he was . . ." She was searching for the right words to express herself.

"You mean he was playing . . . in other words, he was attempting to satisfy himself sexually, isn't that what you mean?" I said.

"Yes, yes, it was very clear what he was doing. Perhaps it would have been best for me to pretend not to notice, but he was looking at me so pointedly that somehow I couldn't stay there any longer, and I couldn't help getting up and leaving the room. I really shouldn't have done it, it's really all my fault . . ."

"Don't worry, you're not to blame. There was nothing you could have done about it," I said, shifting my gaze again to the window outside. Beyond the incinerator, which the neon light had lit up, there was a great patch of darkness. So his main problem was sex after all.

His choice of words in saying that he had killed the

woman with a long weapon . . . perhaps that too was just a symbolic expression of the sexual act. I stared out into the darkness. If that was really true, it meant we would have to go back to Freud's classical theory, which claims that the libido is at the root of all actions. For myself, I preferred the position of the modern psychoanalysts. Then something else occurred to me.

"It may well be, you know, that his escape was not your fault after all," I said.

"But . . . how could that be, Doctor?" she asked.

"Maybe he was only pretending to masturbate, to make you think he was doing it. Perhaps he just did it as a way to get you to leave the room. Of course, it's just an idea."

"Which do you think it was, Doctor?" She seemed genuinely concerned.

"Well, whichever way, we still have a problem," I said. I was struck by the feeling that in Akio Tanno we were dealing with no mean adversary.

The Missing Name

One

Perhaps because of the clear blue sky, the white plaster of the university clock tower seemed blindingly bright. I made my way to the reception desk in the registrar's office and asked for the name of my patient's tutor.

"And what might this be all about, then?" A diminutive clerk wearing black sleeve covers up to his elbows stuck a suspicious-looking face in my direction. All the recent fuss about tuition fees at the university had obviously upset this fastidious little man, who seemed perfectly suited to his bureaucratic job. I pulled out my patient's medical notes and matriculation certificate, and held them out for him to see.

"A student of yours has been admitted to my hospital," I said.

"Hmmm . . . department of psychiatry, is it?" The little man knit his brows as if expressing his displeasure at this unwanted trouble, but as soon as he realized I was a doctor, his attitude rapidly changed.

"Well, I must say we do see a lot more stress in our students these days," he said. "But even though people may be against the increase in school fees, there's no need to go around acting up and involving us staff, is there? We're on very low salaries ourselves." He was simply venting his own frustration on something that had nothing to do with what I had asked him.

But just as he spoke, a young student with her hair tied back in a ponytail came up to the desk and placed a form in front of him. She was applying for permission to use a meeting room. The clerk looked up from his desk.

"Ah, you've come at just the right time," he said. "You attend Professor Miyakawa's seminars, don't you? Would you take this gentleman down and show him where the professor's room is? And while you're at it, that form of yours needs his signature too."

"But why?" she asked. "We've never needed it before. It's only a request for choir practice, you know."

"It doesn't matter if it's practice, or what it is; from now on you need a signature. You've always needed it up to now as well—at least, that's what the rule book says. It's just that we've never insisted on it. Anyway, off you go now and get his signature." The reception clerk was being thoroughly arrogant. His face shone with the satisfaction he felt at being able to use the rules to assert his authority.

"What was all that about?" said the girl as we walked out of the office into the corridor. "Just because we protest the increase in fees, they try and take it out on us." She had a pretty spray of freckles across her face, which she was obviously not concerned to hide with makeup. Her eyes were very large and round.

"Are you practicing something, then, with the choir?" I asked.

"We're doing Beethoven's Ninth," she said. "We're taking part in a choral performance with five other universities at Christmas. It's quite a problem because no one's taking it very seriously. For some reason, at the beginning of summer people just seem to find it hard to settle down, either mentally or physically. I suppose we'll just have to wait till autumn."

She took me to the door of Professor Miyakawa's room in the department of European history, and having gotten the professor's signature on her form, bowed politely and left. As she went she shot a meaningful glance at me, which I found hard to forget.

"How can I help you?" asked the professor. Just like the clerk at the registrar, he frowned when I gave him my card and he saw the medical dossier. The expression on his face said that he didn't want any more trouble with students. Hadn't there been enough fuss over the tuition fees? I let him examine the papers for a moment before getting straight to the point.

"To be frank, we discovered a rather unusual mental block when we submitted this patient to a psychological test." I said nothing about his having been referred to us by the police. I continued the story as if he were my own private patient.

"The block in question involves my patient insisting

that he cannot remember the name of a well-known woman writer."

For a moment, the professor looked as if he did not understand. He was wearing a pair of rimless glasses, his cheeks full and fleshy in an almost feminine way.

"My field is European history, you know," he said. "Is this woman writer you are speaking of a foreigner?"

"No, she's Japanese. She's the author of *A Delinquent's Diary,* and is really quite well-known these days, but for some reason he keeps insisting he cannot remember her name."

"*A Delinquent's Diary,* you say? Do you mean Fumiko Hayashi?"

"That's right. Her work has even been serialized for television, and I suppose you could almost call her a household name," I said.

"In what way does he say that he doesn't know her?" Some color suddenly came to the professor's white cheeks beneath his rimless glasses. He looked directly at me.

"The nurse who was watching him was reading a copy of *A Delinquent's Diary.* One day while she was out of the room for a moment, the book disappeared. When she looked around for it, she found that it had been thrown out the window. When we questioned him, the patient absolutely insisted that he didn't know of any book by a Tomiko Hayashi. The nurse thought it very odd that he repeated the name Tomiko instead of the author's real name, which is Fumiko. That's when I decided to subject him to a formal psychological test, but he was still unable to recall her name. He kept insisting either that the name was actually Tomiko Hayashi, or that he could not remember."

At that moment Professor Miyakawa's cheeks twitched violently. His florid cheeks, testimony to a comfortable lifestyle, went into a spasm that seemed almost like a nervous tic.

"And are you able to explain the reason for this behavior through psychoanalysis?" asked the professor, removing a white handkerchief from his breast pocket and wiping his face.

"Well, we can explain it to a certain extent," I said. "It does remain somewhat in the realm of conjecture, however."

"What exactly do you mean by that? Please explain," said the professor rather abruptly.

"It's probably that the patient does not wish to recall the name Fumiko. Of course he's not aware of this consciously, and it is his subconscious . . ." I had no time to finish my sentence.

"And of what benefit is it to you to investigate that?" The professor's reaction was strange. The twitch in his cheeks became more pronounced, almost continuous.

"Well, it may assist in the patient's recovery. Or again, it may not. It may be a complete waste of time. . . . But in any case, I have no intention of causing anyone any trouble. I would just be grateful if you would allow me to ask you two or three more questions."

"Of course," said the professor. "If it's something that I can help you with I'd be most willing to answer any questions, whatever they might be." He attempted a laugh, but the effect was spoiled by the twitching of his cheeks. I couldn't understand why the professor had reacted in this way simply at the mention of the name Fumiko. I tried a more harmless question.

"I wonder if you could tell me what questions Akio Tanno might have been asked in his entrance exams. Probably sociology or literature questions would be the best."

"What have examination questions got to do with it?" he demanded. "I suppose if you really must know, I have the questions for the exam over here." The professor pulled open a drawer and took out a thick bundle of printed papers that looked like examination questions with their answers. I quickly looked through the questions. Fumiko Hayashi's work did not seem to figure in either the literature or the sociology questions. The only woman writer whose work was mentioned was Ichiyo Higuchi.

"It seems my hunch is mistaken," I said. "I just thought that for some reason he might have been unable to recall the name of one of the authors in his examination papers . . ."

"Well, if you're working on that theory, you should have a look at some of the exam questions for the universities that he might have failed to get into. I'm sure he would have taken the exams for the state universities." The professor started to be more cooperative. He pulled a volume from the shelf entitled *National University Exam Questions,* and flicked through some of the pages.

"No, there's nothing there, not among any of our immediate rivals," he said. "Of course this university is at the top, so I don't really think there are likely to be any other colleges he might have tried and failed to get into." The professor looked very pleased to be able to show off the status of his university.

"Could it perhaps be one of his classmates, a female student with the name of Fumiko?" I asked.

"Let's have a look, shall we?" The professor now pulled out two volumes listing the names of all staff and students at the university and passed one over to me. The list was very thick, and it would obviously be quite a task to find all the names of girls with the name Fumiko from among nearly ten thousand students. I started flicking through the second volume of the register. I couldn't find any girls with a first name of Fumiko, but there were two who had the surname Hayashi. It seemed that the professor could not find any either.

"There's a Michiko Hayashi here . . . I'm sure that's the same name as the actress who played the part of Fumiko Hayashi in the television series," I said.

"Well, if you're interested in her, I'm sure she's a student in my class," said the professor. "Yes, in fact she's the girl who brought you down here just now." A look of relief appeared on his face, and he smiled. Was he perhaps pleased that my visit had not been wasted? But if so, what was the reason for the twitching of his cheeks earlier?

I asked the way to the room where Michiko Hayashi would be doing her choir practice, and left the professor's room. He walked me to the door. "By the way, I did find a male student on my list called Fumio

Hayashi; would that be of any help? There's no telling what these students get up to these days you know . . ." he said.

I thanked the professor for his help. I hadn't noted any homosexual tendencies in my patient. Nonetheless, I did make a note of the student's address in my notebook, just in case. I found myself more interested, however, that the professor had made the suggestion. Halfway down the corridor I turned and saw him still standing with his hand upon the doorknob, a warm smile on his face, watching me walk away.

Two

When Michiko Hayashi saw me coming, she immediately stopped her choir practice to come over and talk to me. She looked as though she was far more interested in the problems of her classmate than in her singing.

"You mean to say you went to see Professor Miyakawa to ask about Akio Tanno?" she asked, amazed. "I've been very worried about him, and what he's been up to, you know."

"Would you mind telling me how well you knew him?" I asked. "I don't suppose you had any romantic involvement with him . . ."

"No, no nothing like that," she said. "Well, I suppose I did like him a little, but he didn't seem at all interested. He joined the choir because I had, but it went no further than that."

"I see. By the way, are there any students in your year who have gotten married while at the university?"

"Well, there's one, but she's much older. In fact she was already married when she became a student, so you couldn't really say it was a student marriage in the true sense."

"Did Akio Tanno have a girlfriend?" I asked.

"Well . . ." She fell silent. The look on her face told me I had injured her pride.

"You see, he's been a bit unsettled recently," she said. "After the choir practice we all go to a café just around the corner from the main gate, and it seems he's been after one of the waitresses—at least that's what some of the others have been saying."

"Would you mind telling me where this café is?" I asked.

"Sure. I was just thinking I'd like to go over there myself and have a hot dog. Their hot dogs are really good, you know." With a spring in her step Michiko Hayashi set off with me. Her clean-looking hair was held tightly with a blue ribbon. She looked like a cheerful girl. I wondered why young Tanno had not returned her love.

But hadn't he said in his statement that he didn't have any friends at all at the university? I couldn't help thinking that there were a number of suspicious things about his behavior. Perhaps it would be simply a matter of unraveling them all one by one. But then again, there was a limit to the time I had. There was just forty-eight hours in which to find my runaway patient.

"How long will he be in the hospital? I'd like to go and visit him, you know." Michiko Hayashi stopped and turned to me as we were about to enter the café.

"Well, as soon as he's more settled you'll be welcome to come and visit." I tried to brush her off with this, but she seemed a little disappointed. I felt that she somehow wanted me to accept that she was more important to him than that.

I soon found out why. Behind the counter stood a girl of around eighteen who looked as if she got most of the attention from the boys. It seemed to me that she was probably Michiko Hayashi's rival. Michiko appeared to have some sort of complex about the girl behind the counter. She probably couldn't bear to think that her classmate was more interested in this girl than in herself.

"Did you ever go out with Akio?" I asked.

"Mmmm . . . no, not really. You see, he was always so shy."

The hot dog machine rotated its sausages right in front of us. The red sausages reminded me of laboratory mice, running around endlessly inside a cage. In some ways it just seemed to be a complete waste of energy.

"Doctor, can you tell me, is Akio just a bit neurotic? Or is he really mentally ill?" She asked me this quite casually as she ordered two coffees, one for me and one for herself.

"It's too early to say, really," I said.

"Doctor, you know sometimes I feel that I'm going a bit crazy myself. Sometimes I suddenly feel that I hate eating hot dogs . . . I feel I can say this to you because you're a psychiatrist, but you know, sometimes I get very sexual feelings when I see a hot dog."

As she said this, she suddenly blushed and looked down. I turned my gaze onto the sausages rotating in front of me.

"That's not necessarily a neurosis," I said. "It's quite normal for people to think like that occasionally. I mean, it's not as if you're obsessed with the thought all day long, is it? When you're doing your choir practice you're fully absorbed in singing, I'm sure, and you're interested in your studies, too, aren't you?"

"Oh yes, I really like doing French studies."

"You know, you're a very attractive girl," I said.

"Really? Thank you very much." Her face brightened. When we finished our hot dogs, she got up from her seat as if she was somewhat reluctant to leave.

"Doctor, I'm sure you probably want to talk to that girl, don't you. So I'll leave you here now. But I hope you'll come and see me again sometime," she said.

"Of course I will." The thought crossed my mind once again that Akio Tanno had missed an opportunity. Such a bright and charming classmate . . . Why on earth had he passed her up? But then again, there really was no accounting for taste.

I ordered a fresh cup of coffee and started talking to the girl behind the counter, the one Michiko had said that my patient had liked. Close up, you could see that she was wearing heavy eyeshadow above her long false eyelashes, and was using a lot of mascara. Her makeup made her look like a model, and her eyes seemed unnecessarily large, giving her a somewhat insecure look.

"Have you heard anything from Akio Tanno recently?" I asked.

"I haven't seen him." She answered my question easily enough. She seemed very friendly, the type of girl who could get along with anyone.

"Do you know where he is now?"

"No, no idea. But who are you, anyway? Are you some sort of shark come to collect his gambling debts?"

"No, I'm just a friend of his from high school. I went to his room but he wasn't there, and someone told me that you might know where he is."

"I suppose it was that girl you were with just now," she said. "You know, she's just jealous of me. She's just putting you on. I've never gone out with any of the boys from the university."

"I see. Well, I'm sorry to have bothered you then. But tell me, have people been here before to try and get back the money he owes from gambling?"

"Well, there was a time when a pretty rough-looking type came in here looking for Akio. You know he really likes betting. As soon as he makes any money he blows it all. He said that he went through all his savings from ten days' work in a single night's drinking. He's treated me to some nice times, too, but honestly, it used to scare me."

She seemed to like talking, and looked as though she wouldn't need much encouraging.

"Did Akio love you?" I asked.

"Did he love me? Well, I don't really know, to tell you the truth." A kind of shadow seemed to pass over her face. I wondered whether she really didn't know.

"So you don't really know him that well."

"No, I don't really. You know men, I can't stand it when they take you out once and then go around acting as though you're theirs." At that moment a young chef in a white apron called out to her in an irritated voice. He was obviously annoyed with our conversation.

"Hey Fumi-chan, that salad's been sitting there for ages, you know." This time the speaker was a man sitting at the end of the counter.

"Oh, sorry." Without the slightest trace of embarrassment, she picked up the salad and took it over to him. I felt a slight tightening in my chest. Hadn't that customer just addressed her as Fumi-chan? I called her over again to me, and asked her name.

"Why do you ask me that? My name? It's Fumiko Kawakami."

"What characters do you use to write Fumiko with?"

"The same as Fumiko Hayashi. I'm sure you know her, don't you?"

For a moment I just stared at her. Could it be that Akio Tanno was so deeply hurt that he couldn't bring himself to remember her name? But . . . at the back of my mind my old doubts came to the fore. Maybe this was just another of his tricks. Could it be his way of putting me onto the wrong track with this Fumiko? Perhaps he had simply pretended that he couldn't remember the name Fumiko.

"What time do you get off tonight? Would you like

to come out with me when you've finished?" I asked, looking her straight in the face. In the time that was left to find Akio Tanno there was no alternative but to follow the footprints he had left behind, even if they were footprints he had deliberately left to confuse me.

"Do you have a car?" she asked.

"Yes, it's a sports car actually," I said.

"Well, you can take me for a drive then, but that's all."

I started thinking where I could get a sports car from.

Three

"Hey, this is a pretty neat car, isn't it." Fumiko Kawakami seemed delighted with the red sports car I had managed to borrow from a friend.

"Where shall we go?" I asked.

"Before we take off, I'd just like to drop in on Akio's room," she said. "If you come with me there won't be any problems. If I go on my own when he's not there, it'll look suspicious."

"What do you want to do there?" I asked.

"You see, I left something behind there," she said.

"So you want to go and get it?"

"Yes, it's a little watch in the shape of a ring. I was given it by a student from Hong Kong as a present."

In actual fact, it suited me very well that Fumiko Kawakami wanted to go Akio Tanno's room. I didn't want to waste any of my remaining time simply asking questions. When we arrived at the room, she got out of the car ahead of me and rang the bell first. She seemed to be quite familiar with the place.

"How often have you come here?" I asked.

"Oh, just once," she replied quite calmly. The landlady remembered my visit earlier in the day, and let us in without saying anything. I decided I would use the opportunity to make a thorough search of his belongings.

"I wonder where he's put it. I hope he's put it somewhere we can find it quickly . . ." she muttered. When she couldn't find her ring on any of the shelves, she went on to open the drawers. I was looking for his diary, or something else that he might have written, but I couldn't find anything. I was sure he must have already been through the room and taken them away.

"I don't believe it! Look where he's put it!" she exclaimed. She was looking into the very bottom drawer. I looked inside, and saw a case containing rifle bullets. The cardboard box with its label was half open, and one of the bullets glinted dully. Next to the bullets was a pair of panties. Fumiko Kawakami grabbed these with an expression of disgust.

"What sort of a pervert is he? . . . Keeping a pair of panties like that, it's disgusting."

"They're yours, aren't they?" I said.

"What do you mean? Of course they aren't mine. I haven't got any black underwear. In any case you can see the initials on them, F.M. It's another woman."

I looked again at the pair of panties and the bullets. I didn't know which was more significant.

"I thought there was something strange going on, you know," she said. "So he is a pervert after all. You know, he invited me back to a hotel once, but he didn't do anything and just cried. That's when I started to think he was strange."

"When was that?" I did my best to sound casual.

"Oh, quite a while ago. Must be more than a month ago, I guess."

"I'd like you to tell me more about that, you know." I placed my hand on her shoulder and looked directly at her.

"What? You must be joking," she said.

"You see, to tell you the truth, Akio Tanno is actually a patient of mine." I took out a card and gave it to her. She looked at me with amazement. But the more I looked into those deep dark eyes of hers, the more I saw the insecurity within.

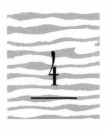

Setting the Scene

One

As before, the water in the pool was stagnant, almost slimy. Given the season, it was obviously going to be left that way for some time to come. Glancing up from the pool to the window of Mrs. Owada's apartment on the sixth floor, I made my way into the building. The concierge announced my arrival over the intercom.

After a short pause, a dry voice answered, "Please show him up." Perhaps because it was through the intercom, her voice seemed to lack all emotion, just like the first time I had visited her. I decided to see what help the concierge might be. "I believe Mrs. Owada had a visit from a young student recently. Do you remember that?" I asked.

"No, I don't. I think you must be mistaken," he answered.

Just to be sure, I repeated the question, but this time

he seemed to take offense. His face clouded over, as if I was accusing him of neglecting his duty. Nonetheless I pushed on, ignoring his feelings. "He was carrying a large box, though, don't you remember?" I said. "Wrapped in department store paper."

"Whenever there is a delivery from a department store, quite naturally we allow it through. Why are you asking such strange questions?" said the concierge, his face reddening in anger.

"I'm sorry, I didn't mean to suggest that anything improper had occurred," I said. "But I see that you still have your finger on the intercom button." I pointed at the concierge's finger. His gnarled, stubby finger was still holding down the intercom switch. I had to accept the fact that Mrs. Owada had probably overheard our conversation. I went over toward the elevator, watching out of the corner of my eye to make sure he had taken his finger off the button. He was muttering to himself. People tend to get angry as a defensive reaction when they are accused of making a mistake.

The inner corridors of the building were lined with blue glass, and lit up by the morning light it looked almost like seawater. I pressed the bell to Mrs. Owada's apartment, but there was a long pause before she came to the door.

"Did I keep you waiting?" she asked when she eventually appeared.

"No," I said diplomatically.

"The zipper of my dress got stuck and I couldn't get it free," she said. The figure that greeted me as the door opened was wearing a close-fitting sweater and a tight black dress. The unsmoothed wrinkles in her dress showed that she had dressed in a hurry.

"You see I always make a point of sunbathing for about two hours in the morning," she said.

"Well, I'm sorry to have disturbed you, then," I said.

"Didn't the concierge downstairs tell you? He's pretty familiar with my daily routine, you know. Apparently he likes to keep tabs on people and find out what they do." She turned a rather cold glance in my direction. I felt she was criticizing me in a roundabout way.

"My patient has escaped from the hospital," I said.

"You mean that student who claims to have delivered a box to my apartment, and says all those odd things?"

"The one who not only says he made a delivery, but also claims to have killed you," I pointed out.

"What strange things young people say these days . . . I'd like to know how he thinks he did it," she said.

"He says he used a long weapon. His motive appears to have been frustration at the absurdity of things."

"Or perhaps it was just that the sunlight was too bright for him. . . . But then it wouldn't have been a long weapon, would it. Meursault used a pistol, after all." She seemed to be testing my reading knowledge, to see if I knew Camus's *The Stranger.*

"I'm afraid I've only read *The Stranger* and *The Plague*," I said, answering her unspoken question.

"I've read Camus's poems, you know," she said, brightening. "His poems about the white summers of Algeria . . . They were a real inspiration to me when I wrote my own volume of poems."

"So you write poetry yourself then, do you?" I asked. I'd never heard her mention this before.

"Well, there was a time when I used to."

"I'd very much like to see some of your work."

"You'd probably only treat it as material for your studies, but I'll show you if you like," she said, leading me into the sunroom. She then went out, closing the door behind her and leaving me alone. The roof of the sunroom had been opened up, and the searing heat of the sun came directly in. There was a large bath towel on the couch, indicating that she had indeed been sun-bathing just before I arrived. To the side of the couch was a large ashtray full of cigarette butts, a big bottle of olive oil, and a paperback in English which she was obviously reading and had put aside. The cover of the book showed a woman's face looking out, her red lips distorted in fear.

Mrs. Owada came back into the room carrying some tea and a bottle of scotch on a round silver tray.

"I prefer whiskey to milk in my tea," she said. "I'm not interested in a balanced diet. I'd rather have a clear head." There was a volume of poetry on the tray. It was called *The White Summer*.

"You can have this," she said. "But I don't want you to read it here. I would feel embarrassed if you read it in front of me."

"Well, I shall be most interested to take it home with me," I said. Suppressing the urge to open the book, I continued to look down at the title, *The White Summer*. Mrs. Owada sat down on the couch. She crossed her legs easily as she did so, and the hem of her skirt rose up, exposing a bronzed thigh which she had just been sunning. It was shimmering from a generous application of olive oil. It occurred to me that she was deliberately striking a provocative pose. This pose and her dark skin stirred images I was struggling to keep out of my mind. I was possessed by a desire that probably any man would have felt, to take off her clothes and stare at her beautiful naked body. The only thing that restrained me was a vague sense of morality, and my upbringing and background. I didn't want her to see this desire lurking in me.

In the end it was my desire to maintain my position as a doctor which prevailed. But I certainly understood the feelings of my patient. Akio Tanno had undoubtedly been instinctively drawn toward her bronzed and beautiful body. Even dogs and cats have such feelings. But instead of controlling their feelings consciously, animals are kept in check by the natural rhythm of a mating cycle. It is man alone who has to learn to control his desires.

Whether or not she was aware of my line of sight, Mrs. Owada languidly uncrossed her legs again, taking an even more provocative pose.

Two

"You say you've met my husband," she said.

"Yes, I've met him twice," I replied.

"My husband had me investigated, you know. But he

needn't have gone to all the bother of paying a large fee to a psychiatrist; he could have just hired a private detective . . . although I suppose his pride wouldn't let him use a mere private detective."

"But you don't understand," I said. "It's not simply a question of your husband's requesting it. My patient sent a summary of the statement I showed you the other day to your husband . . ."

"My husband thinks I was raped by that student, doesn't he?" she said, interrupting.

"No, not at all. He's merely helping me in my investigations. However, he did tell me that the two of you were experiencing some marital difficulties."

"And what difficulties was he referring to, exactly?" she asked.

"He told me that he would like to know more about it himself," I said, wiping the sweat from my face. I could feel our conversation becoming very stilted. Mrs. Owada looked down at the teacup in front of her, before shooting a quizzical glance at me as she raised it to her shapely mouth.

"You see we get on very well sexually," she said." It's not as if either of us experience any frustration in that respect. But because his work as a pilot involves so much stress, I do my best to ensure he gets enough sleep. . . . I've never made any demands on him in that respect since we got married. But I think that most pilots' wives are considerate in this way."

She seemed to be deliberately speaking to me openly and honestly. I got the impression that Mrs. Owada was in fact a very shy person. But somehow, when it came to her husband, she was able to speak like this. I remembered the pretty flight attendant I had seen Mr. Owada with at the airport. Perhaps his wife knew of this woman and felt jealous.

"I wonder if you'd mind if I went on sunbathing," she said suddenly. "If I don't get my daily dose of sun I don't feel right. Perhaps you'll think that neurotic."

Somewhat irritatedly, Mrs. Owada stubbed out the half-smoked cigarette she was holding in her long fingers in the ashtray beside her. She was barely looking in my direction. She left the sunroom and took off her black dress, returning this time in a short robe of the type you see women wearing at the beach. Beneath this she was wearing a bright orange bikini.

"How much longer do you intend to continue investigating me?" she asked.

"But I am not really investigating you," I said. "I simply wanted to ask you a few things face-to-face."

"Well, go ahead, I don't mind. It doesn't even bother me if we talk about personal things, if you like."

I decided to try another tack. "As I was saying, my patient has escaped from the hospital."

"Yes, you told me earlier," she said.

"To tell you the truth, he was being held at the university hospital at the request of the police, and was under observation."

"So he's dangerous." I could detect no note of alarm in her voice.

"Well, he didn't show any tendency to violence at the hospital," I said, "but one can't tell what he will do now that he's escaped. My main fear is that he'll try to carry out what he said in his statement."

"You mean he'll come to kill me with that long weapon . . ." Mrs. Owada looked over lazily at me out of the corners of her eyes from where she was lying on the couch. The sun was dancing on her back and along her legs. I suddenly became aware of something like a thin film at the back of my head. I had had several long nights without any sleep, and the effect was like a drug.

"You know when I stretch out like this I can't help feeling sleepy," she said. "When they give you psycho-analysis, they lay you down on a comfortable couch, don't they, leather or something . . . You know, I've been reading some books on psychology recently . . ."

Mrs. Owada's voice gradually started to sound more distant. As if she were hypnotizing herself, her voice grew weaker and she spoke more slowly. She sounded completely different from the woman with the dry metallic voice who spoke through the intercom.

"It's quite possible that my patient will turn up here, you know," I said. "Should that happen, I'd like to ask you to get in touch with the police immediately."

"But of course I will." Mrs. Owada spoke the words slowly, leaving a perceptible pause between each of them before laying her head down on the couch and breathing slowly as if she had gone to sleep. I stood up and tried to go over to her. But I was beginning to lose sensation in my own body. I somehow brought myself over to the couch where she was lying. It required a great effort.

"Did you put something in my tea?" I asked.

"Yes, I put a sleeping pill in it," she said without looking at me.

"Why did you do that?"

"My husband will be home in an hour. When he arrives the concierge will tell him that you are here with me. But when he presses the bell the door will not open. You see, both you and I will be fast asleep. He will then no doubt jump to conclusions about what is happening here. I want him to suspect you in the same way that he thought that your patient had raped me."

"But you mustn't do that," I said. "You'll only end up hurting yourself. In any case I won't be here when he comes. I'll leave now so that there'll be no misunderstanding."

Mrs. Owada's voice was slurred, but her words were quite logical. She was clearly obsessed with a single thought. That was what scared me.

"You cannot leave," she said. "As a doctor it's your duty to stay by my side. You see I am ill. In any case it will make no difference if you leave. You see, my husband . . ." With these words, Mrs. Owada either was overcome by sleep, or buried her head in the pillow on the couch. I tried to clear my head. So Mrs. Owada was suffering from a kind of mental illness. Was it simply the effects of being cooped up on her own? She probably just wanted to take advantage of my position as a doctor, like a spoiled child. It was hardly likely that she intended to harm me.

I tried hard to make myself believe this. In the meantime, I would do what I could to keep myself awake until Captain Owada returned. I could then ex-

plain the situation to him, and he would be sure to believe me. As I was a doctor, he was bound to take my
word for it.

"Mrs. Owada, do you know a woman by the name of
Fumiko?" I asked. As a way of trying to shake off my
drowsiness, I blurted out the first question I thought
of. In my mind I had the idea that perhaps she might
be linked in some way with this name that my patient
seemed so obsessed with. Mrs. Owada turned her face
toward me again. She looked at me sleepily through her
half-open eyes with their long eyelashes.

"Mrs. Owada, did you by any chance use the name
Fumiko as a pen name when you wrote your poems? Or
can you think of any other association with the name
Fumiko?" I asked again.

She turned her head slowly. Then her head flopped
back down onto the couch, and she failed to rise again.
I started to turn the pages of the book of poems that
she had given me, which I still had in my hand.

The foam on the waves,
The white summer . . .

With increasingly blurred vision I read on, stopping
at random on words like "love," "death." Then my eye
fell on a dedication. It took me some time to take it in,
however, as my mind was already half asleep. I stared
at the lettering, which was in alphabetic script, and
eventually realized that it spelled out the name FU-
MIKO.

I got up and tried to wake Mrs. Owada. At that moment, the doorbell rang. Since it had rung without any warning from the concierge, it could only be Captain Owada. I summoned all the strength that was still left in me in a concentrated effort to make it to the door somehow. I got there and took off the chain.

Three

When I opened the door, however, it was not Captain Owada as I had expected, but Akio Tanno, my patient. A small shock ran through me, which had the effect of sobering me up somewhat. Perhaps because he was just as surprised to see me, his mouth fell open and trembled slightly.

"Akio! I have been looking for you," I said.

"But Doctor, what are you doing here? Have you been waiting here all along because you knew I would return to the scene of the crime?"

"What do you mean, crime? You haven't done anything, you know that. Why don't you come and see for yourself?"

Akio Tanno put his right hand into his breast pocket. Even though he had just run away from the hospital, he was wearing a striped cotton shirt of a fashionable summer design that he had probably picked up on the men's floor of a department store. His hand closed around something in his pocket as if he had a weapon, and then relaxed as if he'd thought better of it.

"This is no different here from the hospital, you know," I said. "Didn't you promise you would trust me? You have to tell me what's going on. What made you come here?"

I was trying hard to make myself sound logical. But in fact I must have seemed either crazy or like someone in a stupor. Akio Tanno had obviously noticed this, since he tried to push past me.

"Doctor, you know I can't just leave it where it is. I have to get it back," he said.

"By 'it,' do you mean the long weapon you talk about in your statement?" I asked.

I was quite tall, and Akio Tanno stood slightly shorter than me. I put my hand on his shoulder. I wanted to talk a little more with him before taking him in to Mrs. Owada. From a clinical point of view, this case was extremely interesting. It could well be that my patient was suffering from a classical castration complex. That might explain why he was insisting on referring to his sexual parts as a long weapon. It is a well-known fact that boys between the ages of four and five are afraid that their penis will be taken away by a girl. However, it was generally only those with a real inferiority complex about their genitals who developed a castration complex when they grew up.

Freud's student Adler postulated the existence of an "organ complex" which when acute led to a "will to power." Since people are keenly aware of their own inadequacies, they are apparently attracted to strong and powerful things to compensate for their weaknesses. I was afraid that Akio Tanno's castration complex would escalate into an attack. He actually believed that his penis had been stolen and had come to get it back.

Tanno made no reply to my question, but pushed me back against the wall.

"Very well then, let's do as you say, and go and look for 'it,' " I said. "But before we do, I want you to promise me you won't be violent, and that you'll do as I tell you."

I washed my face with cold water in the washbasin. I felt that I had now recovered my wits somewhat. Akio Tanno took his hands out of his pockets and let them drop to his sides. His initial excitement at seeing me seemed to have faded. Nonetheless I was aware that there was a very suspicious bulge in his right pocket.

"You've got something in your pocket, haven't you." I said this as gently as I could, but with a wary tone.

"It's a pistol," he said.

"You'd better take it out, then. It's dangerous to be carrying a thing like that around."

"Don't worry, there are no bullets in it. It's just a toy pistol. I was planning to use it to get past the chain when the door opened. If I can just get 'it' back, then I will go quietly."

"Let me ask you again. What exactly is 'it'?"

"I can't tell you, because it would get somebody into trouble. It's a long weapon."

I decided to abandon that line of questioning and get him to take me to the place where he said he'd killed Mrs. Owada with the long weapon.

"Did you leave the long weapon behind here, or was it taken away from you by force?" I asked.

"I left it behind in my hurry to go. There was so much blood everywhere, you see . . ."

"Where exactly was the blood?"

"In the sunroom. You see, I killed her . . ." His shoulders began to shake.

"But if you see that Mrs. Owada is still alive, will you retract your statement? Then you can come back quietly with me to the hospital. If you just come back to the hospital then you will be free to go. You can't keep taking time off from the university, you know; you'll lose all your credits," I said.

At the entrance to the sunroom I again put my hand on his shoulder. I had the feeling that if he saw Mrs. Owada for himself, things might rapidly move to a satisfactory conclusion. At the same time I was worried that the sight of Mrs. Owada in her skimpy swimsuit might upset him.

Bright sunlight filled the room.

"You see, just as I told you, nothing did happen. Mrs. Owada, whom you claim to have killed, is sunbathing over there."

I walked over with him to the side of the couch where Mrs. Owada was sleeping. Her body was glistening with the olive oil she liked to use. With the cool professional touch of a doctor, I lifted her head as she slept and turned her face toward Akio Tanno. Her face felt soft, and she was breathing gently. All I could see from my side was her long black hair.

"There. You see she's alive, and there's no blood anywhere."

I looked up at Akio Tanno and studied him carefully. His face had gone white, and he was staring at Mrs. Owada's face and trembling violently. His mouth hung open, and he was drooling slightly. He was so surprised to see her that for a moment it seemed that he had lost all control of himself.

I let Mrs. Owada's head fall back onto the pillow. As I did so I noticed that her eyes were open and she was looking directly at him.

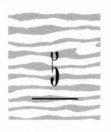

The Twittering of Birds

One

The light streaming in through the blind lit up my bed in the drab hotel room. The sun's rays fell in stripes across the fresh and rather childlike face of Fumiko Kawakami, who was lying beside me.

"So we finally ended up in bed, Doc. You know, I never thought that seeing a psychiatrist would come to this . . ." she said.

"Yes, but you're hardly a patient, so it's all right," I answered somewhat testily.

"Are you angry with me?" she asked. Her thin arm with its jangling bracelets was draped around my neck, the sunlight reflecting off the metal and picking out the gold. It somehow reminded me of Mrs. Owada, her skin glistening with the olive oil she liked to use as she sunned herself in her apartment at Leila Mansions. If I was going to give in to my sexual urges, perhaps I would've done better to have succumbed to the advances she had made to me, and tasted the forbidden fruit. . . .

The night before, I'd taken young Fumiko Kawakami at her word and come with her to this hotel, but now I was beginning to regret it.

"You deceived me, didn't you? In point of fact, you haven't told me anything at all, have you?" I said.

"You see, you are angry," she said. "It's just that there's so much I can't recall now. That's why I'm trying so hard to remember, you know. But if you're just going to get angry, I'll give up and go home."

"Well, just make sure you do remember. If you do, I don't mind helping out," I said.

"But I don't know if I will be able to remember, you know. I'll just have to try and do it exactly the same way as I did with Akio, right from the start . . ."

"But that's exactly what you've been telling me ever since last night, isn't it?" I said. I was on the verge of losing my temper.

"Well, if you're going to be like that . . ." She wrenched free her arm, which had been cradling my neck. I could see her rounded breasts quivering beneath a thin black nylon slip. She could only have been about eighteen. Only eighteen, but with the body of a full-grown woman.

"Your name isn't really Fumiko Kawakami, is it?" I said.

"How did you guess, Doc? My real name is Hiroko Nakazawa." She seemed genuinely surprised that I had asked this, and stared at me with wide-open eyes.

"Well, I just had a feeling, you know," I said. "But

when did you start working in that café in front of the university using the name Fumiko?"

"It was about a month ago. You see I got stoned one night in a late-night restaurant in Roppongi . . ."

"Got stoned?"

"I had some beer with sleeping pills in it. It makes you feel really good, you know, you go all wobbly on your feet . . ."

"And while you were in that restaurant, Akio Tanno came in, didn't he?" I said.

"Well, you see I'd just had a big break-up with my boyfriend that night. My boyfriend is at the university and he's really rich. He drives a really flashy sports car. But he wanted me to do something weird in the car, so I told him to get lost."

"What exactly did he want you to do?"

"He wanted us to get into some heavy petting."

"But you like your boyfriends like that, don't you? So why did you turn him down?" I asked.

"Well you see, he said it to me when we were driving down a freeway, which basically means he wanted me to give him a blow job. I mean, you can't do that when you're driving a car . . . he'd just get all excited and ram the accelerator to the floor, I mean, a car like that, and you'd be doing well over a hundred before you knew it."

"You get into some crazy situations, don't you? It's dangerous, you know, you should watch yourself," I said.

"But you see, all his friends are doing it. But I'm not into that kind of weirdness. I mean, giving men blow jobs—that's something that only a middle-aged woman would do."

I just listened to her without saying anything. I was trying not to let her think from the expression on my face that I understood what she was saying.

"So you had a fight with your boyfriend, and you were getting stoned by yourself when young Akio came in, right?" I asked.

"That's it, he sat at the table next to me and ordered a beer and a curry. I was just getting up to go to the bathroom when I managed to knock over his table, and the rice, the curry, and the beer went all over his trousers . . . that's how we got to talking. When we cleared it all up we went out drinking together and on to another two or three bars."

"So you were sort of making it up to him."

"Yeah, it just seemed that both of us had the same sort of boring lives."

"Well, I expect you'd find that most people would feel that way if you asked them," I said. "It's just that when you grow up you find you don't need to say those things anymore, and you stop being angry about it."

"It's what happened next that I can't really remember very well. I kept telling him I'd pay to have his trousers cleaned. There's this hotel in Yotsuya you can go to where they'll do dry cleaning for you in four hours in the morning, they even press them, you know."

The hotel she was talking about was a large sixteen-storey building built for the Tokyo Olympics.

"And if you want to know how I know a thing like

that, that was the first place that I ever slept with a man, that hotel. He was about forty-three and a director of some company. And you know what he did, he deliberately spilt some soup on my new winter suit, and then said he'd get it dry-cleaned for me, but he just used that as an excuse to get me into the hotel room. And then he forced me to have sex with him when I had my clothes off and was waiting for them to be cleaned. You know, it's hard to resist once you've got your clothes off . . . And I bled, you know, and dirtied the hotel sheets, but in the end I ended up with two new suits out of the whole thing."

She seemed to think that was pretty funny, and put her head against my chest and gave a hearty chuckle. I stroked her soft hair as she lay against me. It occurred to me that those who say that it is nurture rather than nature which decides our development were perhaps right after all, and that there is an adult to blame for every young delinquent.

"So you came here to this hotel room to get Akio Tanno's trousers cleaned?" I asked.

"That's right, this time it was my turn to get him to take his clothes off. But when he'd gotten all his clothes off he started to shiver all over as if he was really cold. So we just hugged each other really tightly. And as we hugged he said it reminded him of all sorts of things. He said that he would tell me all about it as he remembered it. But you see, don't forget I was stoned. So although his stories brought tears to my eyes as I listened to him, I forgot them again immediately. I really couldn't remember a thing when I got up in the morning. So I thought that if I came here and held a man tightly just the same as before, it might jog my memory."

As she spoke there was a slight quiver in her voice.

"Did you make love together that night?" I asked.

"No, we didn't. I was quite ready to, but really we didn't . . . When I reached out to touch him he got angry."

"So it wasn't until the morning that he asked you to take a job at that café around the corner from the university, using the name Fumiko Kawakami?"

"That's right, it was right after the porter brought up his clothes. He got quiet for a while, and then he said he had a favor to ask me."

"Can you really not remember what sort of things Akio said to you the evening before?"

"No, I really can't . . . That's why I keep saying to you, Doc, I want you to hold me in the same way as he did that evening."

I hugged her firm and supple body as hard as I could. I could feel her nylon slip rubbing between our bodies.

"You really aren't getting turned on, are you, Doc? In that case, I'm going to take off my slip. I have to do all I can to help me remember."

I felt a surge of rage within myself at all the moral and social pressures which, even at this stage, were somehow managing to keep my desires in check.

Two

When I got back to the hospital, Motoko Kusano, the young head nurse, had red, swollen eyes.

"Has anything happened to our patient?" I asked.

She knew how I had brought Akio Tanno back from Mrs. Owada's apartment against his will. But she avoided my question.

"I tried to call you at your home so many times last night, Doctor," she said. She was obviously upset. By some sixth sense she seemed to know that I had spent the night with a strange woman.

"I went to see that waitress in the café, the one they say is Akio Tanno's girlfriend. Her real name is Hiroko Nakazawa, but their relationship doesn't really seem to have gotten very far, either physically or romantically. I think perhaps they just happened to run into one another, and, how shall I say, they had a certain understanding for a while."

"I already know that Akio Tanno and that girl have never made love. But you spent the night with her last night, didn't you, Doctor?" She was unable to hide her bitterness. She looked as if she hadn't slept that night, and her eyes were baggy and wrinkled like the creases on her uniform. She had obviously been suffering.

"There's no need to be like that. I just wanted to talk to her, that's all," I said. "Young people like her, street kids, they really have problems, you know. They're already in trouble, but they just won't recognize it. So even if you ask them to, they'll never come into the consulting room of their own free will and lie down on the couch. You have to go out and meet them, there's no other way."

"But that's just your excuse, Doctor," she said, her eyes blazing. "After all, if you didn't say all those fine words you wouldn't be able to let yourself do it, would you? Why can't you admit that you just wanted to sleep with her, that you were just lusting after her young body, but you've never been able to bring yourself to do it before now because you're a doctor."

"What's the matter with you? You really must be overtired, you know," I said. But as I did so, she burst into tears and put her head against my chest. I patted her gently on the back. It was really unlike her to show her emotions so openly.

"What's wrong? Has something upset you? You really must tell me the truth," I said.

"You see, I just had a phone call from that girl, Hiroko Nakazawa," she said. "She begged me to let her speak to Akio Tanno. I told her that it was outside visiting hours and I couldn't put her through to him, so she asked me to give him a message instead."

"And what did she ask you to tell him?"

"She said to tell him that though she slept with you last night, he was the one she really loved . . . I couldn't really understand what she was trying to say, it made me so angry . . ."

"You shouldn't take what patients say so seriously," I said.

"Are you saying that she's sick?"

"Probably. Quite likely, in fact. Anyway, there's nothing between us at all. I did spend the night with her, but all we did was talk."

After calming her down, I went off to see my patient. So Motoko Kusano did love me after all, I thought to myself. But then again, there was Mrs. Owada. There was no getting away from it, there was something mysterious about her. And it was equally true, perhaps, that men were more attracted to women with a secret side to them.

As I came into his room, Akio Tanno was sitting on his bed reading a glossy magazine. He seemed to be looking at a picture of some models in swimsuits. But his eyes were somewhere else, and he was quite obviously daydreaming. He looked for all the world like a distressed little bird who had come home to roost.

"So, how are you feeling?" I asked.

"Not too bad, thanks," he said. His reply was perfectly natural. There really had been a dramatic change in his attitude. It had started the moment he saw Mrs. Owada in her apartment at Leila Mansions. Since then he seemed to have lost the will to keep up his strange behavior. But I still could not explain to my own satisfaction just why he had persisted with it for so long. The only thing that was certain was that he had seen something that, for him, was obviously inconceivable. I sat down next to him and took his hand. His pulse was almost normal.

"You've made an improvement, haven't you?" I said. "If you just get another good night's sleep, you'll be fine. But I would like to know more about the shock you appear to have had."

"Doctor . . . ," he said, looking up at me. His eyes were in dead earnest. "I've been thinking, you know. I think I would like to withdraw my statement."

"Do you mean to say that it's not true?" I asked.

"No, it's not that. It's just that the person I thought I had killed, I mean, who I thought I had shot . . . well, it seems that it must have been a dream."

I let go of his hand. Not wanting to disturb his train of thought, I drew the heavy curtain at the window and switched on the bedside lamp, and went and sat on the nurses' chair by the wall. I thought it was a very good sign that he had started to talk about his dreams.

"I've been having a lot of dreams about being by the seaside," he said. "The sea is a deep blue, shining in the sunlight. When I was a small boy, I often used to go fishing with my father to Enoshima, but this is not Enoshima. And the thing I have with me is not the red fishing rod my father bought for me, but the barrel of a shiny black hunting rifle."

"Did you ever go hunting with your father?" I asked.

"No, we never went hunting. And there wasn't a gun in the house, either. So you see I've never held a hunting rifle except in this dream. Anyway, I'm walking along the seashore with this buttless rifle, and suddenly it changes to a scene in a forest. And there I see a woman. Sometimes it's Mrs. Owada, sometimes my classmate Michiko Hayashi, and sometimes Hiroko Nakazawa, the waitress in the café."

"What are they wearing, these women in your dreams?" I asked.

He thought for a moment before replying. "Mostly they're wearing swimsuits. I can clearly see their arms and legs, but they definitely aren't naked. . . . And you see, I always . . . I always fire the hunting rifle. It goes off with a very loud bang. That's what wakes me up."

"So are you saying that what you said in your statement was just a dream, too?" I asked. "Think carefully. The scene you describe was not by the sea, you weren't woken up by the sound of the gun going off, and, most important of all, you say you left your long weapon behind."

"That's right. That's why I've been thinking about it so much. It is certainly true that I went to see Mrs. Owada at her apartment that day. That's not a dream. It just must be that I raped her that day. When I got home there's no question that I felt terrible about what I'd done. And since then I keep having dreams about the hunting rifle."

He was talking as if he were describing someone else. But at least he had started to interpret his experience, and was trying to persuade himself of it. When he admitted that he had raped Mrs. Owada, I began to feel hope dawning within me.

"I'll tell the police, then, that you wish to withdraw the statement you submitted," I said. I spoke in my most reassuring voice, to try to make him feel comfortable.

Three

That afternoon at the board meeting, a formal decision was taken about Akio Tanno. The hospital's board of directors did not wish to get involved in any more trouble on his account. It was decided to send a formal report to the police saying that, while they had noted schizophrenic tendencies, from now on he would be treated just like any other patient. They were all extremely relieved that he had returned to the hospital.

When the hospital closed for the evening at six o'clock, I was suddenly overcome by a feeling of complete exhaustion. Apart from anything else, I hadn't slept at all the night before.

"Doctor, there's something I want to talk to you about. Would you mind coming back to my apartment?" asked head nurse Motoko Kusano. I was almost relieved to hear her calling across to me from beneath the old ginkgo tree in the grounds of the hospital. She had obviously been waiting for me to appear.

"Well, I'm pretty hungry, you know," I said. "If we go back to your place, will there be something to eat?"

"I've got some beef, so I can make you a nice steak if you'd like. I'll make a special effort if you come, you know; you won't regret it." She had dropped the formal language she used while we were at work, and continued in this relaxed fashion after we reached her apartment. She had quite a small room, but like many

single girls she kept it neat and tidy, and being on the
top floor, there was a very pleasant view.

"Doctor, do you believe Akio Tanno's latest confession?" she asked suddenly.

"Not particularly. I just thought that presenting it
that way would be the best way to get through the
board meeting."

"That's a lie!" she said, angrily. "You yourself said
he made up his statement because he raped Mrs.
Owada. You said that was the most consistent interpre-
tation . . ."

"But you see, I just wanted to do all I could to avoid
his being charged with murder," I said.

"And if we agreed it was rape, that would be all
right, is that what you mean?" she asked, her eyes blazing.

"But Mrs. Owada doesn't accept that it took place,
so legally speaking, no crime has been committed. A
patient is free to say whatever he likes in the privacy of
his own room."

"It just seems to me that you're all trying to avoid
taking any responsibility," she said.

"No, not at all. I just wish we could spend more time
talking to him, that's all."

My mood changed and I fell silent. I couldn't understand why she had brought me back to her room if she
was just going to go on like this. Without her white
nurse's uniform on, she just looked like an ordinary
girl.

"You know, Doctor, I just can't bring myself to believe that Akio Tanno raped Mrs. Owada," she said.

"What do you mean?" I asked.

"You see, I tried a little experiment." She looked straight into my eyes.

"What kind of experiment?"

"Well, you didn't get in touch at all last night . . . and, as I was watching the patient all by myself . . ." She looked down. I had a feeling that I knew what she was going to say. I suddenly felt I had to have a cigarette.

"He was really crying, you know. I couldn't see any sign that he was going to be violent, but I thought it would be terrible if he tried to escape again, or if he tried to commit suicide, so I decided to rub his back for him and listen to his story. I did think that I was perhaps going a little too far, but . . ."

I sat silently and listened to what she had to say.

"After a while he started, very quietly, to say 'You know, I really must have raped Mrs. Owada. . . . ' I felt so sorry for him. He seemed to be really overcome with guilt. Before I knew it I was cradling his head. His hair is so soft, just like a baby's . . . and as I started stroking his hair I suddenly began to feel love for him. He kept on saying how sorry he was for Mrs. Owada, and he buried his head in my chest and cried. He seemed to be terribly upset. And then I started to hate Mrs. Owada, although it was probably just out of jealousy of a woman who can attract men like that. What do you think, Doctor?"

"I'm not really sure," I said, trying to sound as non-committal as possible.

"But as I was stroking his head, I started to feel

strangely alone. And before I knew what I was doing, I found I had undone the buttons of my uniform, just as he wanted. I had put him against my skin so that he could feel me, like a child. He started searching for my breasts, just like a baby."

"I think that . . . that certainly goes beyond what should be expected of a nurse," I said, groping for words.

"I know, but I just had this very strong feeling that he was stumbling blindly in the dark, almost as if he was on the verge of life and death," she said.

"So what was the experiment you did, then?" I asked.

"I just thought that if he wanted to, I was prepared to go all the way with him. But he didn't try to go any further. That's why I . . ." She stopped and heaved a great sigh.

"I took off all my clothes and stood there naked. I took off his clothes as well, to get close to him. But . . . you see, nothing happened."

"Are you saying that you think he's impotent?" I asked.

"That's exactly it. You see there's no way he could have raped Mrs. Owada," she said.

"But maybe he has just become impotent since yesterday," I said.

"No, you don't understand. It wasn't like any ordinary situation. You see, I could feel that he completely trusted me, and if you can't do it under those circumstances . . ."

I stared out the window at the lights of a baseball

stadium visible in the distance. I wished that I too could let myself go as freely. I felt so much more inhibited than Hiroko Nakazawa and my nurses.

"Doctor, you must think I'm very strange. But you see, it wasn't the first time I have had sex and . . . why shouldn't a woman do whatever she likes?" She came over to me by the window. Her pale face seemed so much more attractive in the darkness.

6

Green Duckweed

One

Sitting in the hotel lobby, I was about to light my fifth cigarette when through the fronds of an ornamental plant I spotted the flight attendant, Kyoko Hara, walking toward me. She had changed out of the tight-fitting uniform she'd been wearing when she went into the hotel, and was now wearing a shiny satin Chinese dress.

"I'm sorry to have kept you waiting," she said, "but I had to come by bus, you see."

"Please don't worry about it. I should be thanking you for giving up your time to meet me. I'm sure you must be tired and would really like to get some sleep," I said.

"No, not at all . . . you see, I'm usually so exhausted when I arrive at the final destination that I'm just too tired to sleep. I suppose it's because you're a complete bundle of nerves by then. No, I'd be delighted to have a little chat with you over a drink." Kyoko Hara was standing right in front of me, and I could see the odd flash of her legs through the long slit in her dress.

We moved over to the bar, and I raised the subject of Captain Owada. But it was still early evening and the bar was deserted. As we didn't want the bartender to listen in on our conversation, at first we stuck to small talk.

"It must be hard work being a psychiatrist, isn't it?" she said.

"What makes you think that?" I replied. "It's really not all that difficult, you know. I'm sure that doctors with other specialities have a much worse time of it."

"But it must be quite a responsibility," she said, pursuing her theme. "By the way, do you do psychological tests for pilots?"

"No, I can't say that I ever have."

"Captain Owada said that you'd tested him."

I suspected that she called him Captain Owada out of consideration for her colleagues. If she didn't, the intimacy of their relationship would be all too obvious. I noticed that she'd made the effort to change into her Chinese dress for her meeting with me. But I didn't quite understand why she'd brought up the subject of Captain Owada's test.

"What test was that? I've never been in charge of any formal psychological tests for a pilot," I said.

She made no reply to that. Instead she drained the last of the pink liquid in her cocktail glass. Her slim fingers held the edge of the glass in a very delicate movement. If she had something that Mrs. Owada lacked, it was probably a kind of gentleness, something she herself was probably not aware of. I could well understand why Captain Owada was drawn to this dusky, full-bosomed beauty. Any man would be tempted by the idea of passing some time with her.

"Captain Owada seems to be worried about the results of the psychological test he took when he became a captain," she said.

"Were some of the results negative, then?" I asked.

"No, he was at the top of his group in concentration, patience, judgement, and mental stamina."

"Well, that would seem fine, then, wouldn't it?"

"Yes, but he seems to be concerned that his personal problems might suddenly affect him when making a visual landing, for example."

"By 'personal problems,' do you think he means some sort of subconscious worry?" I suggested. I thought it might help if I rephrased it for her. After some reflection she said, "Yes, that's right," and then suddenly brought the glass that she had been fiddling with up to her mouth. But there was no more of the pink Million Dollar cocktail left in her glass.

I thought quietly to myself that if she were Mrs. Owada, she would probably have been drinking a dry martini with an olive. I couldn't help comparing Mrs. Owada with the flight attendant who was sitting beside me. It was a sign of the anxious psychological state I was in. I obviously was subconsciously jealous of Captain Owada, who had made both these attractive women his own.

After some hesitation she ordered herself another Million Dollar cocktail.

"He says that perhaps he might make an error when landing," she said. "He says that he sometimes has dreams of causing a crash. . . . Do you think this means he has some sort of neurosis?"

"No, not necessarily," I said. "Releasing one's suppressed feelings in dreams is a very normal thing to do. I myself sometimes have dreams of killing a patient." The bartender was listening to our conversation as he crushed the ice for her drink.

"But I think that in Captain Owada's case it's a little extreme," she said. "It's not just that he feels worried about it, it seems that he's starting to believe it. You know he once told me this story of something he said actually happened. In America sometime in 1956 a pilot made an error landing a jet, and it crashed in a field and broke up. Afterward a psychiatrist employed by the authorities investigating the crash looked into the pilot's relationships with women. He found that the night before the crash, the pilot made love to his girlfriend, and for some reason he beat her up on the bed and injured her badly. The girl didn't die, but the pilot thought that he had killed her. That's pretty scary, don't you think?"

"I don't know, that's a pretty common sort of story, I don't think it's particularly frightening," I said. "It's really not much different from the story of a taxi driver who is involved in a crash after having had an argument with his wife—it's the same thing really. The majority of drivers who are involved in accidents seem to have had some sort of argument with their wife before leaving, but that doesn't mean marital conflicts are the cause of all accidents . . ."

I let my sentence trail off. I'd suddenly thought of something else.

"However, if the accident Captain Owada told you happened in America actually didn't happen at all, then that would be a cause for concern," I said.

"Well, that's just it. You see I . . . I checked the company records for that year, and there is no accident of that kind mentioned." She looked straight at me. "There's something I'd like to show you. I wonder if you'd mind coming up to my room."

With this she got down off the bar stool ahead of me, and as she moved, the long slit in her dress opened completely to reveal a glimpse of her white thighs above the dark stockings. As I paid for the drinks I wondered if that had been part of her intention.

Two

Kyoko Hara took me up to a room with twin beds. Both the beds were made up. She took a small package from her suitcase that she'd obviously been keeping very carefully. Inside the package was a paper bag wrapped very neatly in a handkerchief.

"Doctor," she said, "I'd like you to have a look at this."

"What is it?" I asked.

She handed me the paper bag with a very serious expression on her face. Inside was a sheet of airmail paper. But the sheet of paper was blank. It was just a plain white paper. I was quite used to strange behavior from my patients at the hospital. But I could not bring myself to believe that this beautiful woman was deranged.

"And what's the problem with this sheet of paper?" I asked, trying to seem as calm as possible.

"I'd like you to read it. I'm sure that you will understand it when you do, Doctor."

"But there's nothing written on it," I said, puzzled. Just to make sure, I looked again at the sheet of paper. In one corner there was an Italian logo of some kind. I wondered if my concentration was failing me. But in a few moments, I realized why Kyoko Hara had given me this blank sheet of paper.

"If you look at it from above you can't see anything," she said, "but if you hold it up against the light and look through the paper at an angle you'll be able to see."

I placed it against the lamp on the table, and could see the marks of writing on the paper. The paper was indented where it had been pressed on with a ballpoint pen. As I had suspected, what I saw was exactly the same as the writing in Akio Tanno's letter to Captain Owada. The writing was childish, as if it had been deliberately written with the left hand.

"It's been written firmly with the left hand, that's why the letters stand out so much," I said.

"Yes, that's what I thought," she said, looking at me with a very grave expression.

"Where did you get this?" I asked.

"From inside Captain Owada's suitcase."

"This is Italian paper, isn't it?" I said.

'Yes, it's a writing pad I bought for him in Rome. You see I really can't understand why he used the writing paper that I'd given him to write this letter, even though there was plenty of hotel writing paper available. I just want to know who he writes letters to, and why. You see I love him . . . does that make my curiosity unhealthy?"

"And whom did you think Captain Owada was sending it to?" I asked.

"To his wife, or to . . . no, to some other woman, perhaps."

"Did you think it was a love letter?"

"Well yes, I did think so at first, but then when I saw what it was I was amazed. So you see I've known all along that the letter from that student Akio Tanno was written by Captain Owada himself."

"But why would he write a letter suggesting that his wife might have been raped?"

"That's what I can't understand," she said, "but there's no doubt that he wrote the letter to deceive you, Doctor. What is this long weapon that he talks about in the letter? And why would he say in the letter that his wife had been killed?"

I fell silent, and sat on the edge of the bed. I wanted more time to think. I'd had a suspicion that Captain Owada had written the letter from Akio Tanno. When he'd first shown me the letter, I'd noticed the Italian logo in the corner of the letterhead. But I had no idea what that might have meant.

"Why did you decide to show this letter to me?" I asked.

"You see I . . . I'm very afraid. I love Captain Owada, and I'm well aware that he's scared of something. But he won't ever talk to me about it. And more than that, when I see what he's been doing recently it just makes me very worried. I'm frightened . . . you see, I'm worried that he might cause an accident because his mind drifts away from what he's doing right when he's landing a plane, just as he himself fears. . . ." Kyoko Hara held her face in her hands, and suddenly broke down into tears. I stood up and put my hand on her shoulder.

"There's no need to worry. I'm sure that Captain Owada is a very responsible and sensible man. The reason why he told you about that accident that didn't happen is that he's trying to create a safety valve for himself."

"Well, I hope you're right, Doctor . . . but if you don't mind, I'd like you to take this letter with you. I want you to show it to him and say that I gave it to you, and then question him about it. If you do that then I'll feel much better."

"All right, then." I took the letter and walked over to the door to leave.

"Doctor," she said.

"Yes, what is it?"

"Doctor, I'm afraid. If you don't mind I'd like you to stay with me a little longer."

I walked over toward her again. I could see that she was crying, and there were tears running down her cheeks. She stretched out her hand to my neck and brought her lips close to mine. Her lips, shiny with a pink lipstick, were half open.

"Doctor, I'm really afraid . . . but I'm sure that if you just kiss me I'll feel better."

"But I thought you were in love with Captain Owada," I said.

She made no reply. But rising to meet me, she pressed her lips against mine. Her lips were hot, and her tongue tasted sweet. I pressed her against me with my arm around her back. As I released the pressure from my arm, she looked up at me.

"You see, I'm going to meet Captain Owada in this room. We always meet in this room to make love on Thursdays when he comes back to Tokyo."

"What time are you due to meet him?" I asked.

"At three o'clock."

There was another forty minutes to go before three o'clock. I felt slightly insulted, sensing that in a roundabout way she had just rejected me.

"Well, I'd better be going, then," I said. "When I ask Captain Owada about this letter I'll tell you what I've discovered."

"But you see, I'm afraid to meet Captain Owada alone." She said this after I had already turned to go, in a high, imploring voice. I felt there was something about the way she said it that didn't ring true. Perhaps she had once been a drama student. If not, she certainly seemed to enjoy making a scene. But then again, everyone likes to do that to a certain extent. . . .

Three

As I walked out of the elevator into the hotel lobby, I suddenly felt thirsty, and I went over to the bar. In my heart of hearts, Kyoko Hara's words were probably holding me back. Why had she said that she was so afraid to meet with Captain Owada? And why did she seem so obsessed about it?

It seemed pure chance that I made my way out onto the terrace with its garden area beside the hotel pool. Or was I being led, perhaps, by some unconscious force which was guiding me there? From my raised position on the terrace, I noticed that I was in a good position to observe the entrance to the hotel. I thought that when Captain Owada arrived I would like to have a few words with him.

There were several young women in revealing swimsuits lying lazily on lounge chairs with bronzed, oiled bodies. I continued mulling things over as I looked down on this pleasant scene, which was bathed in bright sunlight. But I somehow couldn't focus my thoughts. The blue of the pool was dancing with flickers of golden light.

Suddenly it struck me. I remembered the swimming pool at the building where Mrs. Owada lived, with its stagnant water that hadn't been cleaned out for months. And the sign with its "Members Only" notice. What was it about that pool that was so fascinating?

At that very moment, however, I sensed that there

was something I ought to recognize in the pool in front
of me, right there amid the flickering light. I got
off my stool on the terrace, took off my shoes, and
walked barefoot down to the poolside. The object of
my attention waved a free hand at me and began to
swim over to the side of the pool where I was standing.
I could just catch sight of half a face as it came out of
the water to breathe. There was no doubt that it was
Mrs. Owada.

I watched in amazement as her delicate hands with
their red nail polish gripped the side of the pool, her
shoulders heaving deeply. I searched for some suitable
words.

"You're very good at the crawl, aren't you?" I
said.

"Yes, I love swimming. You can sunbathe, and then
while you're swimming you don't have to think of anything," she replied, stretching an arm toward me. I
took her hand and helped her get out of the water. Her
hand was cold as ice.

"Were you looking for me?" she asked.

"No, not at all, I had no idea that you'd be here. I
just came over because I wanted to look at the pool."
My words seemed to be somewhat of a shock to her.
She looked straight at me with a rather crestfallen face.
Finally she found some words.

"I often come to the beauty parlor in this hotel.
They do full mud baths, you see. I wonder why it is
that women are so interested in makeup and beauty?"
The light reflected off her shoulders as if from pol-
ished bronze. For a moment I felt I was going to faint.

What was this strange feeling of fear that always came over me when standing next to Mrs. Owada?

"Do you know that your husband comes to this hotel?" I asked her bluntly. I had to kill the feeling that was rising within me. I felt I might be starting to feel a kind of love for her.

"Shall we have something to drink?" she asked, ignoring my question rather pointedly. "I'll just bring over my bath towel." But when she came back from the changing room wearing a blue silk dress, she took my arm gently, almost like a lover. "I'm sure there are lots of questions you'd like to ask me. And for my part, I'd like you to act as my therapist. How much do you charge for an hour of your time?"

"I wouldn't want to charge you anything," I said, "if you really are prepared to speak honestly with me . . ."

"No matter how many lies your patients may tell, as a doctor I'm sure you see through them," she said.

"Not always. There are times when you don't," I said, trying to sound noncommittal.

As we came into the hotel lobby she withdrew her arm from mine. I looked around the lobby and was relieved to find that I couldn't see Captain Owada anywhere.

"I have a room in this hotel, you know; shall we take our drinks up there?" she asked. She took me up to the room she had taken for the day. It was the room right next to room 707, which Kyoko Hara had brought me to earlier. At first I thought I must have been mistaken, but when I looked at the number again there was no mistake. Could this be just a coincidence, I wondered.

I couldn't decide whether I should say anything about the room next door.

This was also a twin-bedded room. The covers were still on both beds. Mrs. Owada didn't say very much until the waiter brought up the drinks from downstairs. Then she kicked off her sandals, and standing on tiptoe in her bare feet, she peered out the window. I stared patiently at the olive in my martini which the waiter had brought, as if waiting for a patient to calm down. I was sure she would break her silence sooner or later.

"I always take this room when my husband is staying here in the hotel," she said. "All the foreign pilots from his airline stay here when they're in Tokyo. One of the flight attendants takes a room here too."

"Do you mean Kyoko Hara?" I asked.

"You're well-informed, aren't you?" she said.

"Do you expect to see your husband here soon?"

"He's already here. That's why I take this room in the hotel. Perhaps there's something wrong with me that I'm doing this." She placed her hand on her throat with an elegant motion. It seemed rather as if she had a pain in her throat.

"Do you want to say that you are jealous?" I asked.

"I'm not conscious of being jealous. You see, I don't love him . . . but I can't stand it unless I'm in the room next door when those two are making love."

"Can you hear sounds from the next room?" I asked.

"Oh yes, you can hear; you can hear very well. I can get a very clear picture in my mind of exactly what expression is on his face." She stood up and went over to a cupboard at the side of the room and opened the door. Inside was a small tape recorder with an amplifier and an earpiece.

"You see, I listen through this. You must think I'm very strange."

I looked directly at her. Somewhere deep inside me there was something that made me want to believe what she said.

"Mrs. Owada, I don't believe you," I said. "I'd like you to stop this pretense, going to all this trouble to rig up equipment like this. It's no good trying to make me think you're obsessed with sex."

As I said this she fell silent, but came toward me. She stood on her toes in her bare feet just as she'd done when she was looking out the window. Small though she was, when she put her arms around my neck and stretched up, her lips came close to mine. Her lips were half open and I could see her white teeth.

"I read the book of poems you gave me," I said. "Who is the Fumiko whose name appears in the dedication?" I asked.

"Never mind talking, just hold me. Fumiko is my dead sister." She said this very casually, but I could feel her whole body trembling in my arms very slightly. Was this the trembling of a little girl embracing a man for the first time? Or was it simply a sign of how much she was looking forward to sex?

Was she really a sexual obsessive? Had she in fact taken Akio Tanno into her room like this and kissed him on the lips, as it said in his statement? With all these doubts swirling in my mind, I brought my own lips closer to Mrs. Owada's. As I touched her lips, the image in my mind's eye was of a surface of water, with duckweed floating on it like the pool outside her apartment. In my imagination the sign standing in front of the pool fell over with a crash.

Traces of Water

One

Passing through the university gate and looking up at the white face of the clock tower, I felt a real sense of relief. I somehow had the feeling that this was the only place where there was still something pure. Although I couldn't really explain to myself why, in my mind I had the image of something like a spring of cold water bubbling up and frothing over. It showed the extent to which I felt I had peered into the depths of human ugliness and depravity in the past few days.

I was shown into Professor Miyakawa's office, where I sipped a cup of tea that his young assistant brought for me as I waited for him to arrive.

"The professor always likes to let his classes run over a little, so I hope you won't mind waiting a few more minutes. I'm sure he'll be back very shortly," she said before leaving the room. She had a surprisingly warm voice, considering her rather prim, un-made-up face.

The professor's office was lined with many foreign books, as one would expect from his specialization, which was European history. I reached for a biography on Napoleon and looked at the face of this little man from Corsica, whom the Viennese psychologist Adler once characterized in the phrase "a man who took power to compensate for the small size of his organ." In the picture on the cover of the book, the eyes of this infamous man seemed filled with the melancholy of either a tyrant or a madman.

I searched my own conscience again for hidden feelings of inferiority. Could it be that the thing I was about to do was no more than compensation for some complex or other? Or should it perhaps simply be called an act of love . . . ?

While I was thinking this over the professor silently entered the room. As on the previous occasion, a pair of silver cuff links glinted in the cuffs of his white shirt.

"I'm sorry to have kept you waiting. Did you find something interesting to read?" he said.

"I was studying this picture of Napoleon. There's something of this man in my patient, you know."

"Ever enthusiastic for your work, I see. By the way, on the subject of that student of mine, Akio Tanno, although you were good enough to inform me that he has now left the hospital and is coming to the university, I've yet to see him at any of my classes."

"Is that so? He told me that he was attending classes . . ." I let my sentence trail away unfinished.

The professor sat down in a large chair in front of

his desk and lit his pipe. There were a number of things that I would have to confront him with now. It seemed that he somehow knew this.

"The last time I came to see you about my patient, I asked you whether there was a student here by the name of Fumiko Hayashi. Do you remember?" I said.

"Of course I remember." The professor was looking down at his pipe and answered without looking over toward me. Despite this, I could see that there was no reaction of any kind anywhere on his face.

"At that time I was asking you specifically about students, but could it be that a lady called Fumiko Hayashi is actually part of your own circle of acquaintances?" I asked.

The professor made no reply, so I continued.

"For example, someone very close to you indeed . . ."

The professor's face suddenly twisted up. He had obviously not been prepared for such a blunt question.

"It is . . . it is the name of my wife," he stammered. He seemed to be searching for words as he answered me.

"Her maiden name was Fumiko Hayashi, was it not?" I said.

"That's correct."

"So why didn't you tell me that when we met before?"

"There's no reason why my private affairs should have any bearing on my seminar students, is there? You are being offensive. I wasn't hiding anything from you. And in any case you aren't a policeman." The professor was now shaking with anger, as if he could barely control himself.

"That is quite true, but my patient is one of your students. Is it possible that Akio Tanno might have seen your wife for any reason at all?"

"Absolutely not! How could he have? What on earth are you trying to say—are you trying to break up my family? You're just trying to dig up a scandal, aren't you?"

The professor had already stood up from his chair. His face had gone quite red, and he was pointing an accusing finger at me. It looked as if some deep anger which had built up in him over many years was now exploding, although I couldn't help feeling there was a certain theatricality about his outburst.

I hastily abandoned my inquiries and made my way out of the professor's office. I had suffered such a shock myself that I couldn't have gone on. My question had been no more than a hunch, after all. A hunch, but I'd certainly gotten more than I'd bargained for.

Fumiko . . . wasn't that the name of the person Mrs. Owada had dedicated her volume of poems to? It was also the name that Akio Tanno had a fixation about. The amazement I felt was like that of a small child who discovers that he has built a castle just by moving building blocks around at random. Should I now just come to a stop in front of the gate of this castle, or should I take a new interest in this fact, which was starting to have all sorts of unexpected implications?

Another of Adler's anecdotes came to mind. Imagine, he said, that two young men, one an introvert and the other an extrovert, are traveling together in a foreign land when they come upon a beautiful castle. The introvert feels sure that such a wonderful castle will be heavily guarded and he will never be allowed inside, and so hesitates to go on. In complete contrast, the extrovert's first reaction is to take an optimistic view of things. He feels sure that there is a beautiful princess in the castle who will be happy to welcome them and encourage them to stay the night.

Whistling as he goes, the extrovert cheerfully proceeds to the gate of the castle, but the introvert is sure that something terrible is going to happen, and follows him with a heavy heart. When they actually get inside the castle, however, contrary to both their expectations they find it is a military museum. An old custodian appears and starts to tell them a long story. The extrovert is terribly disappointed, and is irritated with the old man's tedious stories. On the other hand, the introvert is delighted that there are no guards to arrest him and that somebody is there to tell him all about the museums that he likes so much, and really enjoys himself.

Was I an extrovert, or was I the introverted young man, I wondered? Whichever I was, the feeling I had standing in front of my building-block castle was one of fear and deep insecurity. To try and calm myself down, I made my way to the students' smoking room down the hall, and had a cigarette.

Two

The water in the pool in front of Mrs. Owada's apartment was as foul and stagnant as ever. The dead brown leaves floating on the surface were a sign that autumn was well on its way. For some reason, someone had pasted a white notice on the members-only sign saying "Not in use this summer."

I had a cigarette by the poolside, and then made my way up the fire escape at the side of the building. As I had thought, the door on the sixth floor of the fire escape was not locked. When I pushed gently on it, the heavy metal door opened without a sound, as if by magic. I went in and stood in front of the apartment nearest the fire escape, which was Mrs. Owada's. After a brief hesitation, I pressed the bell.

Before pressing the bell I had tried the door handle, but the door did not open. When Mrs. Owada appeared, she seemed upset.

"What do you want? Will you please phone up from the lobby before coming to visit," she said in a cold voice, glaring at me. She seemed completely different from the woman who had looked up at me at the hotel swimming pool with such passion in her eyes. I felt a chill of despair run through me.

"I'm sorry to have bothered you. I just suddenly felt I wanted to come and see you today," I managed to say.

"You mean without any specific reason?"

"Yes, there's no particular reason. But if there was

one it would be . . ." I couldn't bring myself to finish.
Mrs. Owada heaved a deep sigh. She was obviously re-
acting to my unspoken words.

"What do you mean, 'if there was one . . .'? I hope
you're not putting on airs."

"I suddenly felt that I had to come and check
whether the door on the fire escape was locked or not."

"And did you?"

"Yes, as I had suspected, the fire escape door is not
locked. You can get in from the outside and come
straight up here without going through the lobby."

"You shouldn't be able to do that." Mrs. Owada continued to look me straight in the eyes. Though they
were completely devoid of emotion, I couldn't help
noticing a slight movement, like the faintest ripple, in
the deep, dark pool of her eyes.

"Someone who lives on this floor has just accepted
delivery of an electronic organ, you see," she said. "It
wouldn't fit into the elevator so they had to bring it up
on the fire escape. I'm sure they must have just forgotten to lock the door again." As she spoke, a softer and
more gentle expression came over her face.

Her slightly cold, hard, yet beautiful face now relaxed into a charming and seductive smile. There was
something about this new expression which reminded
me of a mother calming a spoiled child. I felt as if my
whole body was sinking into a deep swamp. There was
something about her words and the expression on her
face that was difficult to resist. I was determined to
hold her off at all costs. I dug my fingernails deep into
the palms of my hands.

"But I'm sure it is you who leaves the door to the fire escape open," I said. "And not just this time, but on several other occasions. . . . Sometimes you've kept it open almost every day. Akio Tanno must have come up the fire escape, as well. That's why the doorman downstairs never saw him."

"You're starting to talk more like one of your patients than a psychiatrist," she said. "That's pure and utter supposition on your part. If you don't believe me, come into my sunroom. You can hear the electric organ they have just brought in from the window there." With a beckoning gesture, she invited me in, still continuing to treat me like a small child.

When I entered the apartment, I couldn't believe my eyes. The white decor I was used to had been transformed into bright orange, with furniture and fittings to match. The curtains, the couch she used for sunbathing, everything was orange. And the sunroom itself was filled with a strong, almost acrid smell that seemed to be coming from the rubber plant and the other plants which she had placed in the corner. It smelled like a French cologne, and indeed there was a large bottle of cologne sitting on the flower table.

"I see you've redecorated," I said.

"Yes, my doctor always used to tell me that I should change the decor and the perfume in the room once every six months, for a change of mood. Not that this doctor was a psychiatrist, of course," she said in a somewhat cynical tone. I let this pass as a joke, and quickly looked around the room. If I was right, there must be a visitor somewhere in the apartment. I was working on

the theory that she had opened the door to the fire escape to bring someone up without their having to go
through the lobby. But there was no sign of anybody
else having been in the sunroom, which she used as her
living room. In any case the small ashtray was unused,
and the only butts in the large standing ashtray obviously had her lipstick on them. I felt a twinge of disap-
pointment, and looked over at Mrs. Owada. As always,
there was a graceful smile on her lips.

"Have you been doing any sunbathing lately?" I
asked.

"Yes, I have."

My eyes shifted from her face to the orange couch.
There was a large bath towel spread over it. Under the
bath towel I could see something like a large black
stain.

"May I sit down, please?" I said.

"Please make yourself at home . . . I'll bring some
tea."

As Mrs. Owada left me alone when she went into the
kitchen, I went over to the couch and picked up the
bath towel. The couch seemed to be damp with water. I
suddenly had the idea that it was sweat. The mark left
by the water on the couch was exactly the shape of a
pair of thighs. I thought to myself that it was probably
her sweat, and as I did so I found myself blushing.
Why was I fantasizing about this? I imagined Mrs.
Owada's lithe body swimming gracefully in the pool
like some flying fish.

But she had probably had a shower and then lain
down on the couch. How stupid of me to have ever

imagined that there could be anybody else in the room. If anybody else were in the apartment the only other place they could be hiding would be the bedroom.

From where I was, I could see through to the kitchen where Mrs. Owada was standing. Opposite the kitchen door I could see a white enameled refrigerator. It was a large type of fridge of the kind you see in restaurants in American films. Japanese people generally don't like to use such large fridges. As I was thinking about this, somehow this large, sparkling-white fridge gave off a strong impression of cleanliness. It was probably because I remembered how Mrs. Owada had had the sun-room all decorated in white when I first visited her apartment.

"Have you met up with my husband yet?" she asked as she came back into the room with the tea. Her tone was quite friendly.

"No, not yet." I looked her straight in the eyes as I replied. I was still torn by my feelings. Perhaps the only thing left for me to do was to play my trump card.

"The person I went to meet today was not your husband but Professor Miyakawa, who teaches at Akio Tanno's university. Do you know Professor Miyakawa?"

"No." She turned her head slowly as she replied. She still had that gentle expression on her face.

That can't be true! I shouted to myself. *You must know the professor's wife. In fact it's even possible that she came to visit you here today* . . . I looked over at the closed door of the bedroom and stared at it.

"I read your book of poems *The White Summer,* which you gave me," I said, changing tack.

"And what did you think?"

"Well, I found the poems very interesting, but the thing I found most impressive was the fact that you'd dedicated the book to a person called Fumiko."

"What a strange person you are," she said, keeping her face completely expressionless as she poured me a cup of tea.

Three

"I hope there are no sleeping pills in the tea this time," I said, only partly in jest.

"No, no, don't worry. I haven't put any in this time."

Despite her assurance, I somehow had the feeling that without sugar, the tea was bitterer than it should have been. I decided to press on with the question of whom she had dedicated her poems to.

"The wife of Akio Tanno's professor at the university is also called Fumiko," I said.

"And what significance does that have?" she asked.

"While he was in the hospital Akio Tanno showed an extreme aversion to the name Fumiko. The name was a kind of psychological block for him and we could not make any progress with it. He kept insisting that he couldn't remember the name of Fumiko Hayashi, the author of *A Delinquent's Diary,* which every high school student should know."

Mrs. Owada was silent.

"This shows that a woman named Fumiko was somehow an obstacle in his mind. So I decided to see if there were any women named Fumiko in his immediate circle of friends and acquaintances."

"And were there?"

"Yes, there was a waitress who works at a café near the university gate. But she could hardly be said to have been very involved with him."

I paused, but Mrs. Owada said nothing.

"However, today I discovered that the wife of his professor is also called Fumiko. It seems that for some reason the professor concealed this from me. When I asked him about his wife he exploded with rage."

"But what has all this got to do with me?"

"Because I suddenly had the idea that the Fumiko to whom you dedicated your book of poems was the professor's wife."

"I have no knowledge of a professor's wife called Fumiko Miyakawa," said Mrs. Owada. As she said this, she stood up and turned her back to me.

"I think that Akio Tanno knew that the professor's wife had come to visit you here. Something happened which had a profound effect on him. . . . Mrs. Owada, I think you're hiding something from me. Even as we speak, I think you're hiding someone in your bedroom, aren't you?"

I shouted these last words at her back. She turned around to face me. There was anger blazing in her eyes.

"You are completely crazy. You are the one who should be seeing a psychiatrist. If you're crazy enough to believe that, then go look for yourself." With this, she picked up the large bottle of cologne that was on the table and with all her strength threw it at my feet. The bottle didn't break, but the top flew off and the perfume spilled all over the floor.

Then she opened the bedroom door, so I immediately went in to have a look. There was nobody in the bedroom. There was the Owadas' large double bed, and that was all. As one would expect in the bedroom of a married couple, there were two soft-looking pillows placed together on the bed. I stood there blankly, drained of all energy. She moved around to face me. In her bare feet, her head barely reached my shoulder.

"Look at you, you're just like a jealous little boy in love." Her voice had lost the roughness it had had earlier, and was smooth and sweet as honey.

"You may be right. I'm really not sure myself. Sometimes I think I ought to do what Akio Tanno did. Then I would just come up here without any hesitation and knock on the door of your apartment. If you'd just send me away like a stray dog, then maybe I'd come to my senses."

"Well, are you satisfied now?" she asked. "You see there is nobody here. My husband won't be back until tomorrow."

As if to prove what she had said earlier, I could hear the sound of an electronic organ drifting into the room, a simple melody but at the same time somehow melancholy, repeating itself over and over. I suddenly felt the weight of autumn upon me.

Although I couldn't see it from the bedroom, I re-

membered that the swimming pool would now have
been out of use all summer. For no reason at all, the
image of a sign came into my mind, posting a strict
warning: 'Nonmembers are not allowed around the
pool.'

Mrs. Owada suddenly closed her eyes. I could just
glimpse the well-formed teeth within her beautiful lips.
It almost seemed the mouth of somebody else. I suddenly thought that she must be very lonely. I had the
feeling that I was being pulled relentlessly into a deep
pool. I placed my hand on her back and put my lips to
hers. It felt like ten minutes or twenty minutes or even
all of eternity. I was trying to cross a borderline that
I was not allowed to pass. Once again the image of the
notice at the pool floated up before my eyes. At
the same time, it was somehow both Mrs. Owada's
face and Akio Tanno's face. As I fell with her onto the
large bed she pushed me away forcibly with both
hands.

"I'm a married woman," she protested. "I won't
deny that I'm fond of you, but I don't want to get involved in anything more than this." She said this in the
same dry tone that I'd first heard through the intercom.
I felt my desire for her vanish, together with the great
divide within me.

"I don't want you to come here again when my husband isn't here," she said. "The Fumiko I dedicated
my book of poems to is my dead sister. I don't know
any professor's wife . . . and when my husband is away
nobody comes up to this room except me."

I came to my senses and left the bedroom. The

damp patch was still on the couch in the sunroom, with the bath towel across it.

"The couch is very wet, isn't it," I said. I tried to mention this casually, and was not particularly expecting any reply. I just couldn't bear the silence.

"Yes, I just came back from swimming in the pool . . ."

"What do you mean, the pool down below?"

"Yes, of course."

"What, that dirty old pool where you can't see the bottom—you mean you swim there?"

"Why ever not?"

At first I thought she was joking. But I suddenly felt a chill run through me. Her face was perfectly calm, even smiling. But her eyes had somehow lost their focus, and she was staring into the distance. It was like when a person loses their memory, or is trying their best to suppress a powerful memory from the past. It was a dangerous sign.

I suddenly felt like looking at the pool. This pool had somehow remained stuck in my mind from the very first time I visited this building. The bottom of that filthy old ugly pool . . .

Mrs. Owada watched in silence as I left the apartment.

8

Diving In

One

I t was my third visit to the university. The white clock tower was swathed in a light mist in the autumn rain. It somehow reminded me of psychiatric case studies which suggest that the onset of mental illness is influenced by the weather. . . .

With this thought running through my mind, I made my way to the café beside the entrance to the university. As usual, the grilling machine was slowly rotating its sausages on top of the counter.

"Is Fumiko Kawakami in today?" I asked the sullen-looking girl who was standing behind the counter.

"She's been fired because she kept taking time off."

"Do you know where she's working now?" I asked.

"No idea. With a girl like that, you know she won't stay long wherever she goes."

Fumiko Kawakami obviously hadn't been popular with the other girls working at the café. They must have been put off by her provocative clothes and her direct way of doing things. I ordered a hot dog and a coffee. If I couldn't find Fumiko, then my little experiment would fail at the outset.

As I was drinking my coffee, the door to the café opened and in came Michiko Hayashi. I assumed that she must have been looking for me, as she immediately came and sat on the stool next to me.

"You've just been over to the university, haven't you, Doctor," she said. "No matter how hard I shouted your name after you, you just kept walking on, so I followed you in here. There's something I want to give to you."

Even though she was sitting beside me, she was still breathing quite heavily. I could see beads of sweat forming at her hairline with its childish wisps of hair.

"What is it, then?"

"I've got something that I want you to give to Akio Tanno. I hear that he's been confined to your ward, Doctor."

"Who told you that?"

"Why, Professor Miyakawa, our class teacher, told us when he came into the room this morning."

"That's very strange," I couldn't help interjecting. Professor Miyakawa should have known full well that Akio Tanno was no longer at the university hospital. I wondered why he had said such a thing to his students.

"Akio is no longer at the hospital, you know," I said. "The observation he was under at the request of the police ended last month, and he left the hospital. He said he wanted to go back to the university, so I let him go."

"But he hasn't been to any classes," said Michiko.

"Yes, I know. We had a call today at the hospital from his parents. They got a telegram from him ten days ago asking them to wire him some money so that he could go home, but they haven't heard from him since."

"So nobody knows where he is again, then?"

"It looks that way, doesn't it," I said.

"I bet he's gone off with another girl like that Fumiko Kawakami. If he keeps on like this he's going to get thrown out of the university, you know. After all the things we've done to help him, too. . . ." I could see tears welling in her eyes, and her hands tightened on the magazine she was holding.

"You know once a person has grown up, there's no way you can really help them," I said. "If they don't want to help themselves, then it's just a waste of time."

"Oh, but it is possible to help people, you know. You can help them by saying encouraging things."

"You really are in love with young Akio, aren't you?" I said.

"Well, I don't know if I actually love him or not. I just don't think I can bear the thought of not seeing him again. But I've been stupid. I should've slept with him. I should've taken off my clothes like a waitress in a café and thrown myself at him." Michiko Hayashi broke down into exaggeratedly hysterical sobbing. It was somehow like watching an actress getting carried away with her own performance.

"Anyway, then, you have no idea where Akio might be now?" I asked, hoping it might calm her down.

"No, no idea at all," she said between sobs. "I thought he was at the university hospital. He sent a poem from the hospital for the choir newsletter, and I made the committee promise to publish it. You see, his poems are so good, they're so honest. Some of the other committee members didn't like it because they said it was too difficult to put to music . . . but I think that lyrics are much more important than the melody that goes with them."

She wiped the tears from her eyes and looked up at me for sympathy. I asked her to tell me some more about the magazine in which Akio Tanno's poem had been published. Under the heading "Writing Lyrics and Music for Performance" were three poems contributed by members of the choir. Akio Tanno's poem was the last, and it was short, cryptic, and clearly quite difficult to put to music. Nonetheless, there was something very powerful about it. It was very suggestive, like the poems often written by psychiatric patients.

> *I don't want to fly away anymore*
> *I don't want to fly*
> *Like a piece of shrapnel or a bullet*
> *I just want to keep on bobbing up and down*
> *I want to be the duckweed bobbing in a pool*
> *If I could*
> *The face of a beautiful woman*
> *Would shine down on me like the sunlight*

"What do you think of that, Doctor? They all say it's too passive, a sort of antiwar thing. I suppose you could say that isn't exactly positive, but . . ." She broke off, uncertain how to express herself.

"Could I take a copy with me?" I asked.

"Of course. I'd like to get a copy to him somehow."

As I stood up to go, I noticed that Michiko was staring at the sausages going around on the grill.

"Doctor, I'm still having dreams about sex with boys, you know. I get so embarrassed when I wake up," she said, gravely.

"Don't worry about it. Everyone has those kinds of dreams, you know." I thought to myself how Michiko was obviously from a happy middle-class home where they never had to worry about money for the school trip, the cost of school lunches, or anything like that.

Two

As I went into the late-night restaurant in Roppongi, I suddenly couldn't remember whether I should be looking on the left- or the right-hand side. I racked my brains. Yes, it was definitely the left-hand corner in which Fumiko Kawakami said she had first met Akio Tanno and talked with him.

The restaurant was divided into two separate sections, to the left and right of the entrance. Neither she nor Akio Tanno was in the left-hand side. But when I made my way over to the other side, I found Fumiko Kawakami sitting with her back to me, next to the window by the street.

"Do you always sit here?" I asked, taking the empty chair opposite her.

"Sure I do. And who are you?" she said.

"I'm the doctor from the psychiatric unit where Akio Tanno is. Don't you remember we met once before?"

Fumiko looked intently at my face, but her large black eyes lacked focus, and she seemed to be somewhere else. I was quite sure that she'd taken several sleeping pills with her beer. She tried to stand up, but as she did so she knocked over the beer on the table in front of her. The foam from the beer ran out all over the table.

"Oh yes, Dr. Uemura. Yes, that's right, you took me off to a hotel somewhere, didn't you. . . ." She raised her face toward me and attempted a smile, but her expression soon crumpled into a frown, like an old woman. She keeled over in front of me and slumped on the table, with her head in the beer.

"Hey, pull yourself together," I said, lifting her head. "Is this the table where you first met Akio?"

"Yes, that's right, we always meet here."

"But you told me that it was the window seat in the corner."

"Did I, is that what I really said?"

She sat up and tried to get another look at my face before waving her hands in front of me with their bright-red nail polish.

"I don't remember saying anything like that. I told you it was the left-hand side we sat at, I'm sure of that, the left side."

She patted the top of the table with her right hand.

"Here, over here. This hand, the left hand."

"That's your right hand, isn't it?" I said.

"Oh, is it. . . ." She looked up vacantly at me. A waiter in a white jacket appeared and wiped the table with a cloth. The letters that she had traced in the foam of the beer on the table disappeared in a flash. I didn't know whether it was the effect of the sleeping pills, her confused memory, or whether she was deliberately lying to me.

"I'm looking for Akio Tanno again, you know. Have you seen him recently?" I asked.

"No, I haven't. I'm looking for him myself." Suddenly she pulled herself together and stood up. "Let's look for him together," she said.

"But where shall we start?" I asked.

"Anywhere in the world. . . . Except that he might be going to a party tonight, you know." She took two or three steps forward, and leaned heavily on my arm.

"What's this party you're talking about?" I asked.

"It's in an apartment in Harajuku. It's one of those parties that anyone can go to."

She called a taxi and somehow managed to give the address. As soon as we got into the taxi she put her head on my shoulder and dozed off. I could smell the scent of lavender on her skin, a fragrance which thrilled me and filled me with despair at the same time. I had very strong memories of that smell. I was quite sure it was the perfume that Mrs. Owada had been using.

The apartment in Harajuku was very large, and obviously belonged to a wealthy Chinese businessman.

The house sitter, an exchange student from Indonesia who was looking after the apartment in the owner's absence, had opened it up to his guests. Fumiko Kawakami seemed to be able to enter freely, and nobody bothered to check on me since I was with her. There were already about twenty people standing around in the living room or out on the terrace, all drinking cocktails laced with sleeping tablets. They were mostly quite young.

"Hey Doc, grab yourself a drink." Fumiko brought me over a drink, but I just put it to my lips for a moment before putting it aside.

"Seems like Akio hasn't shown up. I met him here the other night, you know. I thought I'd go home with him, but one of the rules of this party is that you can't stay with the same partner all the time. After a while Akio went off with some other girl. She seemed a little wild to me." She was speaking quite seriously now, as if jealousy had somehow brought her to her senses.

I left her for a moment to walk around on my own, picking up a cocktail glass as I went. I walked around among the other guests, taking a good look at who was there. I wondered if the people who came to these parties really had such a good time. It seemed to me that they were all trying desperately to fill up some bleak, empty space inside them. Otherwise, how was it possible to explain the behavior of a girl who was leaning against the bar in front of me, idly dropping tobacco from a cigarette into her cocktail glass? She looked up at me and laughed, and drained the glass with the tobacco in it in a single gulp. I thought to myself that I had seen saner behavior in some of my patients. There was a storm brewing at this party. A storm blowing up in the mind . . .

"You can't go in there all by yourself, you know." The odd accent stopped me in my tracks. A dark-skinned man with sunglasses was standing at the half-open door of what appeared to be a bedroom.

"Do you have to have a partner, then?" I asked him. He nodded silently at me, and then shoved me back roughly. I was suddenly overcome with curiosity. Could Akio Tanno be in that room? I went back to the bar where I had seen the smiling girl dropping tobacco into her drink, and pointed to the bedroom.

"No, not there. Mommy would be cross with me," she giggled.

"I only want you to go in there with me for a moment. How old are you, anyway?" I asked.

"It's rude to ask a lady her age." She giggled again. "I'm sixteen, if you really want to know."

I turned away, but the girl came after me. She wore a fashionably tight skirt that stopped about eight inches above her knee. Her fishnet stockings emphasized the shape of a body that was very well developed for her age.

This time the man with the sunglasses at the bedroom door said nothing. His face was quite expressionless. Perhaps he had already seen too much to be shocked by anything now. As we entered the bedroom I could see young couples rolling around on the floor like a scene from the sixties in Greenwich Village. I sat down on the floor with my new partner.

That was when I noticed that there was a film being projected onto the ceiling. But it was not the pornographic film that I had expected. It showed inkblots arranged in symmetrical patterns, rather like the Rorschach test used in psychoanalysis, but blown up large for projection. With the Rorschach test, a subject may see a bird, a dancing figure, or a face, depending on their personality type. Their reaction to an image, and whether they see the whole of a figure or only part of it, is determined by their psychological makeup.

The images being shown on the screen were changing at a steady speed, sometimes dramatically, sometimes very subtly, the colors varying through reds, blues, and purples according to the shape.

"What on earth is this?" I asked.

"It's supposed to be people having sex. It's been done by some graphic artist who tries to express music visually. They say if you keep on looking at it, you'll start to feel really great, like you've gone to heaven or something . . ." The girl I'd come into the room with seemed to know all about it, but didn't seem particularly interested in it, for all that.

All around I could hear animal-like breathing noises. I looked around me, but I couldn't see anyone who looked like Akio Tanno. Then, from the light of the projector, I noticed a couple at the foot of the bed. The man looked like a student. But when I saw the woman's face, I felt a sharp shock, almost like a pain. It was the flight attendant, Kyoko Hara. What was she doing in a place like this, when she said she loved Captain Owada so deeply? I somehow managed to stop myself from

calling out to her. It was hard to tell whether the expression etched on her beautiful face was pleasure or
pain.

Three

Returning to the bar in the living room, I ordered a
drink. I was still in shock at having seen Kyoko Hara at
a place like this. What on earth was she doing here? But
then again, I could well ask myself the same question.
Fumiko Kawakami was out on the terrace dancing with
some blond-haired American. She already looked very
unsteady on her feet.

After my third drink, I finally saw Kyoko Hara
emerge from the bedroom. Like a person coming from
the bowels of the earth into the light of day, she nar-
rowed her eyes and made for the bar where I was sitting. Apparently she hadn't noticed me there. She
ordered an orange juice, and drank it down as if she
was dying of thirst. Her face looked as though she'd at
last come back to the real world. Nonetheless, it
seemed that the pleasure and abandonment she had
been enjoying was still lingering in every part of her.

"Do you come here often?" I asked her suddenly.

Kyoko Hara turned around to face me. As she looked
at me her eyes widened briefly in surprise, but soon re-
assumed the vacant look I had seen earlier.

"So, we meet again," she said.

"Why are you hurting yourself like this?" I asked.

She took out a turquoise-studded cigarette case from her bag, and removed a cigarette with an impatient gesture.

"If I stay by myself I just start to go crazy, you know. When I come here I can forget everything," she said.

"But what are you trying to forget? Don't you love Captain Owada?" I asked.

"You see, when Captain Owada landed today at Haneda Airport he overran the stopping point by some twenty feet."

"I'm no expert on these things, but it seems to me that an overrun of twenty feet is really not much to get upset about."

"It is in his case," she said. "He's extremely particular about such things, almost obsessively so. Up until today he has never stopped a plane more than ten feet beyond the stopping point at Haneda Airport, you know."

"But who actually measures these things?" I asked.

"He told me himself, so there's no mistake. You know he's very worried about something. Sometime or other . . . I just know that sometime soon he's going to have an accident. . . . A lot of people are going to die, and he will die with them. . . ." Her shoulders were heaving. Her vacant look had given way to something like hysteria.

"You're making too much of it," I said. "We couldn't go on living if we went around making every little mistake into the cause of an accident."

"But we can observe a pilot's psychology from the

way he controls his aircraft. That's scientific enough, isn't it, Doctor? You said so yourself." She looked up at me hopefully. One of the buttons on her blouse was missing, revealing a glimpse of her full bosom.

"May I ask you something personal?" I asked.

"Please do." She looked up at me provocatively, as always.

"Have you been avoiding Captain Owada recently? You didn't meet him at the hotel room, did you?"

"Yes I did," she said, but looked away as she did so. It made me feel there must be some rift between her and Captain Owada.

"Doctor, I want you to promise not to tell Captain Owada that I was at this party," she said.

"I won't say anything about it," I promised.

She turned her back to me, picked up her leopard-skin bag, and walked over to the door. I was just trying to decide whether or not to follow her when Fumiko Kawakami came up to me.

"Hey Doc, it's boring here tonight, let's go. Have you slept with that girl you were talking to just now?"

"No, not at all. She just happens to be someone I know. I don't really want to meet people at a place like this, you know."

"But it's not as if you're doing anything wrong. I don't like adults, you know. They start to have such strange guilt feelings about things." She walked off ahead of me as if she was angry.

As we left the apartment, I couldn't see Kyoko Hara anywhere in the broad main street that stretched out ahead of me. I suddenly felt I should have talked more to her. She might have run into Akio Tanno at the party.

"Hey Doc, you don't feel like going swimming, do you? I've got this strange urge to go and do something stupid." It seemed that Fumiko Kawakami had recovered from her little mood."

"What do you mean?" I said, "It's much too cold. You don't want to catch a cold, you know. In any case, where can you go at this time of night?"

"Akio told me there's a swimming pool at the apartment house where he killed that woman. I've always wanted to go there, you know. You know where it is, don't you?"

"You know Akio hasn't killed anyone," I said sharply.

"If he says he did, I believe him," she said. "I believe everything he tells me."

She managed to get me into a taxi, and made me give the driver the address of Mrs. Owada's apartment. As we approached it, the eight-story building where she lived loomed out of the darkness like some medieval castle. The only light to be seen was the light from the concierge's office and the red lights on the fire escape.

"So where's the pool, then?" she asked.

"Now listen, we're just going to look at it," I said. "I tell you, there'll be trouble if you go swimming."

It obviously wasn't going to be much fun swimming here at this time of year. For a start, the water was very cold, and furthermore, it hadn't been changed for at least a year, and was sure to be stagnant and filthy. I stood at the poolside and looked up to Mrs. Owada's room. Thinking of her all alone in her room made me ache with a pain I could not express in words.

Suddenly I heard a loud splash. Fumiko Kawakami had waited for me to look away and had jumped into the pool. Her green dress and white underwear were lying where she'd thrown them at the side of the pool. From the entrance to the apartment house I could see a man who looked like the concierge approaching with a flashlight in his hand. I had the nasty feeling that we were in for trouble.

Just then a light came on in the Owadas' apartment on the sixth floor. A silhouette looking very much like Mrs. Owada appeared at the window.

Mirror in the Night

One

I was feeling very depressed. Exactly why I was feeling that way, though, I did not fully understand. If anything, it was probably the expression I had seen in Kyoko Hara's eyes at the party in Harajuku. There wasn't the slightest flicker of hope on her face.

When I'd first met her at Haneda Airport, I had the strong impression that she and Captain Owada were very much in love. I'd thought of her and Captain Owada as a couple, with Mrs. Owada somehow left to one side. But if Kyoko Hara had really given up on her love for Captain Owada, then I would have to revise my simple theory of a love triangle.

What worried me most was her concern about Captain Owada having an accident. It was the fact that Captain Owada himself seemed to believe he was bound to have an accident sometime that was so disturbing.

The night wind had already turned quite cold. It was the kind of night where you could be forgiven for having a premonition. A poet would perhaps be moved to write a poem. I simply felt a wave of anxiety pass through me.

I made my way to a Chinese night club in Ginza. I went and sat in one of the cheapest seats, at the back on the second floor, and waited for Kyoko Hara. After I'd gotten through my third highball, she finally appeared on the stage in front of me, and sang a song. She was wearing a gold Chinese dress with a deep slit.

The stage in the club was set up to move from floor to floor like an elevator, starting on the ground floor and moving up. By the time the performance was drawing to a close, the seats on the third floor were almost completely empty. Apart from myself there was only a young couple and a student buried deep in a French text. Although the lights were on her as she stood on the stage, she immediately noticed when I raised my glass to her. Five minutes later she came and sat down in the seat next to me.

"What are you doing here?" she asked.

"I've begun to realize that I should have listened more carefully to what you were saying about Captain Owada, and your theory that he's going to have an accident."

I looked down at Kyoko's Chinese dress with its deep slit. I could see her smooth skin through it. I suddenly remembered the expression I had seen on her face as she brought a mouthful of ice cream to her lips in the airport bar.

"I'd like to buy you an ice cream to make up for it," I said.

"If you like," she said. "Although this voucher allows me a half-price performer's discount, and it'll be a waste if I don't use it. But tell me, how did you know I was performing here?"

"One of the girls at that party in Harajuku told me. It seems they all think of you as a singer there, don't they?"

"Well, I've always been very fond of singing, and when I finish a shift as a flight attendant my nerves are always on edge. So they let me come down here and sing to relax. It's just a lark, really," she said.

"The man who runs this place is the owner of that apartment in Harajuku, isn't he," I said. She didn't answer, but instead lit a cigarette with her gold French lighter. I could guess the meaning of her silence. It was her performances here as a singer which had led to her being invited to those parties. She'd obviously started going to them after she'd given up on Captain Owada.

"You sing very well," I said. "Your voice is very attractive, you know, it's so warm and sensitive . . . I really did feel moved listening to you." I was complimenting her, but it was not just hollow praise. I really had felt touched.

Remember how I used to love you
And how you used to love me . . .
Life has washed away our love
Like footprints washed away in the sand

The lyrics were sentimental enough, but I felt that she sang them with feeling.

"I'm thinking of giving up my job, you know," she said, suddenly.

"What for?" I asked.

"Well, there are various reasons." She looked down. The star sapphire in the ring on her left hand caught a ray from a wall light, and sparkled deeply. A ring on the third finger on the left hand usually means an engagement. Perhaps because she caught my line of sight, a smile flitted across her face.

"Oh, that. It's just a lucky charm. It doesn't mean I'm engaged or anything," she said.

"Forgive me if this is somewhat indelicate," I said, "but did you ever partner Akio Tanno at one of those Harajuku parties?"

Kyoko was silent. But she looked straight back at me as she answered. "You see I . . . whenever I go there I am always so stoned . . . I just don't remember who I have been with."

As she said this, what I saw in her eyes was a flicker of despair more than embarrassment. Though neither of us made the first move, we both stood up to go.

Two

When we left the night club, she had changed back into a more conservative ochre-colored suit. Perhaps because of it, she seemed even more sophisticated than usual.

"Today is Captain Owada's day off, isn't it?" I said.

"Yes it is, but he's stopped flying regular passenger flights. He's been put in charge of special cargo flights to Vietnam. He requested the transfer himself." With this brief reply, she placed her delicate hand on my arm in a very natural gesture.

"Aren't you seeing him anymore, then? You always used to meet him at the hotel and spend some time together, didn't you?" I said. I remembered the time I had seen her walking so excitedly in the hotel on that summer day, and the sparkling eyes of Mrs. Owada as she swam in the blue water of the hotel swimming pool.

"You see, Captain Owada has been avoiding me recently, even on his days off," she said.

"When did he start doing that, I wonder?"

"I couldn't tell you precisely . . . but I suppose it's been at least three weeks now," she said. I could feel her grip on my arm tighten very slightly. We were now walking toward Hibiya Park. We could see the silhouettes of several couples in the park, which was lit up with neon light.

"I wonder if you could tell me how you started your affair with Captain Owada," I said. "In other words, exactly what role he played in your relationship. . . ."

"I always thought how terrible it was for Mrs. Owada, and I really felt sorry for her. Of course, I still feel that way . . . but you see by the time we became lovers in the full sense, he told me that he and his wife had been strangers to one another in sexual terms for some time."

"That would be about a year ago, I suppose?"

"Yes, that's right; in fact I asked him why he didn't get divorced. He never gave me a really clear reply to that, but it seems his wife didn't want a divorce."

I had an uncomfortable feeling hearing her say this. Mrs. Owada had insisted to me on my visits to her apartment that her relations with her husband were quite satisfactory. I remembered her saying this on a number of occasions. I was sure she had meant that she was satisfied in a sexual sense.

I continued walking in silence for a while.

The other question was why Mrs. Owada should have gone to all the trouble of recording her husband's love affair at the hotel. Whatever way I looked at it, I could not find an explanation for her behavior that satisfied me.

"Were you and Captain Owada aware that Mrs. Owada always took the room next to you in the hotel where you stayed?" I asked.

"What?" She was incredulous. "I don't believe you. Why on earth should she do such a thing?" I could almost feel the shiver pass through her body.

"Perhaps because she wanted to express her love in some way," I said. "Even if only in the form of jealousy . . . but I don't believe that she was simply obsessed and wanted to know what her husband and his lover were doing. In my opinion, she is a much cleverer woman than that."

"You're quite in love with Mrs. Owada yourself, aren't you?" she said.

"Well, I certainly have a deep sympathy for her, I

think." But as I said this, I could feel I was beginning
to enjoy this conversation too much for its own sake.
After all, what mattered now was to find Akio Tanno
again, and nothing else.

"You see, I'm looking for my patient," I said.
"There's been absolutely no sign of him for the last
week, ever since that party. I'm afraid he may have suffered some new psychological trauma at the party.
What I'm most afraid of is that he has experienced a
form of sexual trauma. For a young man like him, any
sexual experience can completely alter his entire
world."

"You think I slept with Akio Tanno at that party,
don't you, Doctor?" she said.

"I'm very much afraid so. You see, his whole attention is focused on Mrs. Owada. He is attached to her to
the point of obsession. When he realized that there was
an insuperable barrier between them, he may have
transferred the object of his affections to a substitute.
A normal person would obviously try to find a way
around it. Experiments with guinea pigs confirm this.
But once they give up trying, a small number of the
guinea pigs turn around and run in the opposite direction after banging their heads against the wall for a certain amount of time. They transfer their attention to a
hypothetical object behind them. They become mentally unbalanced, and instead of going for a carrot, they
start biting the bars of their cage."

"So you think he has substituted me for Mrs.
Owada?" she asked.

"I don't know, but I do get that feeling."

"But how could he have known I was Captain Owada's lover at that party the other night? I mean, as far as everyone else was concerned I was just a singer. And even assuming that Akio Tanno knew I was Captain Owada's girlfriend, how would he have been likely to react?"

"He insists that he shot Mrs. Owada dead when he went to make a delivery from the department store. But in fact Mrs. Owada is alive and well. This leads me to the conclusion that when he uses the phrase 'shoot with a gun,' it in fact has a sexual meaning for him. When I went to see Mrs. Owada, Akio Tanno was trying to get into her apartment again. I noticed that he had a toy pistol with him, which was when I realized that his true purpose was a sexual one, and that he did not in fact intend to kill her. Since that time he hasn't bothered Mrs. Owada. So it seems that he has managed to transfer his affections."

"Onto me, I suppose you mean."

"It could well be."

"But if in fact I did sleep with Akio Tanno at that party . . . well, it would be a cause for celebration, wouldn't it?" She looked at me somewhat cynically.

"Not in this case. You see, he doesn't really want to achieve the object of his desires. If he has the illusion that he has reached his goal, he'll collapse. I want to make sure he keeps trying a little longer. That way we may be able to find a way of helping him."

"And if he collapses, what then?"

"He will lose consciousness and go into a coma-like state, which is the secondary stage of his depressive illness."

"Well, that is rather worrying . . . you see, there's another of those parties in Harajuku tonight, and he may well be there. But in actual fact I don't think that I could have let him go that far. I mean, I know I don't remember it very well, but . . . with all the other men I was involved with . . . you see, I never took my underwear off. I mean we did get quite carried away, but not to that extent. . . ."

Her voice trailed away and I could see that she was staring into space. She had both hands on my arm, and held on to me tightly.

Three

There were already a number of sports cars parked outside the building in Harajuku. Kyoko Hara and I went into the darkened apartment where the party was being held. She still had her hand on my arm.

"It doesn't look as if he's here. Let's wait a little while to see, and if he doesn't show up we can just go," I said, as I walked across with her to the bar and ordered two dry martinis. Behind the counter stood the Indonesian exchange student, mixing a drink. He had strong, muscular arms and a physique to match, and he shot a quick glance toward us as we stood across the bar. He was obviously sizing Kyoko up.

"Do you know if a girl called Fumiko Kawakami is here tonight?" I asked him. He shook his head rather slowly and gave me a sullen stare. I could feel his eyes following me as I turned my back on him and headed to the room where they were showing the film with Kyoko on my arm.

Inside the room, abstract patterns were being projected onto the white ceiling just like the last time, and some frenetic modern jazz was coming out of speakers on the floor. I raised the martini to my mouth, and held the olive between my teeth.

"Doctor, please, I'd like to ask a favor," Kyoko said after a while. Her voice sounded flat and listless. "Please don't leave me here, will you? I want you to stay with me, and be my partner tonight."

"That's all right by me," I said, but to tell the truth I wasn't absolutely sure what she meant.

"You see, I've just had one of those spiked drinks. I'm sure I'll start to get high in a moment. When I do, I know I won't remember anything about what I've done afterward. So I want you to watch me all the time, and see if I take Akio Tanno as a partner."

As she said this, she also took the olive in her own glass and held it between her teeth. She then turned slowly and pouted her lips at me. She was obviously trying some sort of experiment. She was trying to make me a witness of what she did while she was not aware of herself.

I settled down on the floor and watched patterns of colors on the ceiling with a vacant stare. Had Mrs. Owada really succeeded in driving a wedge between her husband and his lover? I wondered. And if so, how she had done it . . .

At that moment, I felt a female arm drape itself around my neck, interrupting my train of thought. Kyoko Hara was trying to push herself onto me, and had brought her lips close to mine. It was clear that she was not her normal self, and her breathing was irregular and rapid.

"Shall we go out and get some air?" I said.

"No, I don't want any of that. I want to stay here," she replied. She was speaking quite mechanically. After she spoke she slowly keeled over and collapsed beside me. She seemed to be having difficulty breathing. With her right hand she was pulling roughly at the buttons of the suit she was wearing.

"God, it's so hot in here . . . I'm absolutely boiling in this jacket. This room is like the Sahara in the mid-day sun . . ."

I could see the white fullness of her breasts beneath the black bra she was wearing as they rose and fell with her breathing. It was almost as if Kyoko Hara had transformed before my eyes from a sophisticated and elegant woman into a complete slut.

Again she came close to me with her lips half open. As I touched her soft lips, there was a strong taste of olives. Before I knew it, I had my arm around her and was pulling her onto me just like the other couples in the room. I could feel her body twitching occasionally in a convulsion. She was obviously enjoying herself in her drug-induced fantasy. But in the end, although we embraced passionately, she still kept her underclothes on. After about an hour she suddenly came to, as if she had been woken up suddenly from a deep sleep, and stared directly at me.

"Is that you, Doctor?" she asked, blinking slightly.

"Well, you did say you wanted me to stay with you," I said.

"But . . . I thought you were Captain Owada," she said. She looked almost embarrassed. "I'm afraid I've been using you as a substitute, just like you were saying earlier. I'm so sorry."

"But you were almost asleep, in fact. It seems to me that you probably don't do any of the things you imagine."

"Well, you can't go by what you saw today, you know," she said, standing up rather shakily, and then made for the bar, where she drank an orange juice. A smaller, friendlier-looking student was working at the bar now in place of the one who had been there before.

"Why not?" I asked, following her to the bar.

"That other guy must have put something in my drink. You see, he's just jealous. That's why things are different today from usual."

"Do you usually change partners when you're in that room?"

"I don't really know, but every time I realize what I'm doing, I seem to be in the arms of a different man . . . it always leaves me with an unpleasant feeling, like I've got sand in my mouth or something."

I had just put my arm around her shoulders and was steering her out toward the balcony, when the door of the apartment opened and Fumiko Kawakami burst in, surrounded by a group of boys. She appeared to be completely drunk. Despite that, she recognized me immediately and shouted out, "Hey, Doc!" in a loud voice.

"Hey Doc, Akio's swimming in his girlfriend's pool, you know."

"What? Since when?" I asked.

"Well, he's been there for about a week now, I'd say. Seems to like diving, or something. There's a whole bunch of police been down there and pulled him out."

I suddenly had a very unpleasant feeling in my bones.

Four

There was a police car parked next to the pool outside Mrs. Owada's building, with searchlights playing on the surface of the water. The members-only sign at the side of the pool had been trampled to the ground by the comings and goings of police and onlookers.

"What's going on here, please? I'm a doctor," I said, going up to the nearest policeman.

"We don't know whether he got drunk and just fell in, or whether he killed himself, but we've just pulled the body of a young man out of the water over there," he said.

"Have you identified him yet?" I asked.

"He seems to be a student. Looks like he's been at the bottom of the pool for about a week, so he won't be very easy to identify, you know."

I went over to the side of the pool, where a body was lying covered with a sheet. Introducing myself to the policeman who was guarding it, I lifted up a corner. Just as I had feared, it was my patient. Green duck-weed was smeared across his pale face. I remembered a line from the poem he had written: "I want to be the duckweed bobbing in a pool."

How ironic that now seemed. He had obviously been hinting at what he was planning to do.

I did some hard thinking about what could have driven him to commit suicide. After a while, I went over to the apartment house. I could hear the uniformed doorman at the entrance of his office, talking excitedly to a man who seemed to be a detective.

"Even though it's so cold, just the other day some young woman jumped into the pool and had a swim," he was saying. "I can't understand what gets into them. They must be absolutely crazy . . ."

I silently crossed over to the elevator, made my way up to Mrs. Owada's apartment and pressed the bell. After about five minutes, a pale-looking Mrs. Owada came to the door in a red gown. The bright red of the gown seemed oddly inappropriate in the circumstances.

"Has something happened downstairs?" she asked in a low voice.

"Yes. They've found a body in the pool," I said.

"What? How horrible."

"The person they found was young Akio Tanno," I said, keeping my eyes on her to see if I could gauge her reaction.

"But how terrible. . . ." She said this with feeling, but abruptly turned her back on me and walked toward the sunroom.

"Where is your husband?" I asked.

"This morning he said he was going hunting, and he hasn't been back since," she said.

"Does your husband like hunting?"

"Yes, he usually goes once or twice a month."

"So that means you have a hunting rifle at home, then."

"No, he always borrows a friend's. His friend has a license."

Mrs. Owada walked through the sunroom and pressed her face against the window, as if trying to see down to the ground below. The bright light from two searchlights was still playing across the stagnant water of the pool. For a moment I had the horrible thought that the pale body of a woman would come floating up to the surface as well.

The light in the sunroom was off, and Mrs. Owada's pale face was right in front of me. A strong smell of expensive French perfume, suggestive of the bedroom, wafted across in place of the cologne she had been using before.

"You know, young Akio came to visit me again about a week ago. I kept the chain on the door and didn't let him in, but he said he'd come to apologize for all the trouble he had caused. He told me he had lied about firing a rifle, and what he really meant was that he had just been fantasizing about me and exciting himself. I felt really sorry for him. He seemed to be all shut off in his own world, the sort of person who just goes on making things worse for themselves." She turned back to the window and stared down at the pool as if mourning for him.

After a while she said, "I'd like you to stay with me. Please talk to me a little longer. I feel so alone, you know . . . Perhaps I should have let him sleep with me after all."

"But why didn't you call me immediately when Akio Tanno came to visit you?" I asked.

For some reason I suddenly felt that I didn't believe a word she was saying.

10

A White Mist

One

A thick mist was spreading slowly over the airport. I put my coat collar up as I walked along the runway. The journalists ahead of me were talking excitedly among themselves.

"It's really strange that Captain Owada did that, you know. He should be quite used to foggy airports in Europe. Why on earth should a mist like this be the cause of an accident?"

"He must have been overtired."

"Overtired? Captain Owada hadn't flown for the last two days."

"There's something wrong with the flight control here, you know. Apparently when he took off he was given only three minutes' notice. Anyway, it's a foreign airline company, so what's a Japanese pilot doing making cargo runs to Vietnam?"

The journalists had obviously been doing their

homework, but none of them seemed to have gotten a hint of Captain Owada's personal problems. For some reason I felt relieved at that. But I was biased by my feeling that it was best to leave the Owadas to sort out their own problems. After all, it was quite normal for a doctor to wish to protect his patients' privacy.

When I reached the end of the runway, I could see the aging jet that Captain Owada had been flying to Vietnam leaning to the left and burning. The ground was covered in white foam from the fire extinguishers.

I stood back from the crowd of onlookers who had gathered around the firefighters trying to save the burning plane, and stared at the flames licking up through the plumes of black smoke. It was then that I noticed Kyoko Hara in her flight attendant's uniform, standing against the headwind with a white scarf holding her hat. I couldn't make out the expression on her face. As soon as I'd found out that she wasn't on Captain Owada's plane, even though it should have been obvious since it was a cargo plane, I'd felt a strange thrill of emotion. I walked over to her, and almost without thinking put my hand around her shoulders.

"So you weren't with him, then," I said.

"No . . . but I wish I had been, so we could have died together," she answered. "Why did all this have to . . . you see, it happened just as he said it would."

"Is Captain Owada still on board the plane then?"

"Yes, there's no hope, they'll never save him now. And there's another man, his Canadian copilot, on board as well. It's just lucky they weren't carrying any American soldiers . . ."

As she finished speaking, her self-control seemed to go, and she buried her head in my chest and started sobbing. She'd told me again and again that Captain Owada was sure to have an accident. Should I have paid more attention to what she was saying, and been more worried about Captain Owada's state of mind? At the same time, though, I could hear a voice telling me that it wouldn't have made any difference. I felt a deep sense of helplessness as I stared at the flames reaching skyward.

After awhile I turned to her again. "There's really no point just hanging around here, is there?" I said.

"No, you're right," she said. "After all, he'll be no more than a heap of bones by now. I expect he didn't even feel anything. But I wonder how much people really feel when they die."

She seemed to be saying this more to herself than to me. Her voice was strangely weak.

"I'm sure he was already unconscious by the time the airplane started burning," I said.

"But when it was on the way down he must have been thinking of something. That's what I would like to know . . ." She said this in a tearful voice, struggling to hold back her tears and clinging onto my arm pathetically. It felt as if it didn't matter who, she just wanted to be with somebody tonight who was living flesh and blood.

"I'll take you home if you like," I said.

"But I don't live in Tokyo, you know. You see, I always used to stay at the hotel with Captain Owada." She suddenly looked at me with a very serious expression. "I wonder if you wouldn't mind taking me to the hotel. And then I want you to make love to me. I really don't like going to places like that party in Harajuku. I just went there because I thought I could forget myself. I really just want . . . I want you to love me."

We picked up a taxi outside the airport, and drove off to the downtown hotel where she and Captain Owada used to meet. That was where she always stayed in Tokyo. We made our way up to the twin-bedded room with our arms still linked. I couldn't help thinking that the man whom she used to go to this room with was now inside a burning jet, and was having his name broadcast across the nation on radio and television. What on earth could it all mean?

When we got to the room, she took off her uniform as if it was the most natural thing in the world, and went to take a shower. While she was in the shower I went to the window and stared down blankly at the empty garden. I wondered what Mrs. Owada would be doing now. I wondered if she already knew of her husband's death, and how she would be coping. Would she be searching for a man to comfort her, just as Kyoko Hara was? Or would she be shutting herself away, and crying inconsolably? I stubbed out my cigarette, and began to take off my tie.

We lay naked together on the bed in silence. That brief moment when everything is forgotten passed over us like a storm.

When we had finished, she said, "You know, I think that after all he probably committed suicide. I can't give you a definite reason, but I just have that feeling."

"But do you think that Captain Owada would have

taken somebody else with him like that, even though there weren't any passengers?" I asked.

"You see recently, even when he was with me, the expression on his face always seemed to say he couldn't stand it anymore," she said. "He used to tell me he was at the end of his rope. He felt he was being completely crushed by his problems."

"That isn't enough of a reason," I said.

"But you see, I loved him. You always understand the person you love." She said this as if talking to herself, and in a moment she was asleep, cradled in my arms.

When dawn came, I was awakened by the sound of a news broadcast from the bedside radio. I'd forgotten to switch it off before going to sleep. The newscaster spoke in the usual serious tone.

"The military jet which crashed at Haneda on take-off last night continued to burn till one o'clock this morning, but the bodies of the crew have now been identified. Although it had previously been thought that only the captain and his copilot were on board, a third, unidentified body has now been discovered. At the moment it is not possible to confirm whether it was a member of the crew, but there are suggestions that this unknown third person may hold the key to the cause of the accident."

I suddenly felt a chill down my spine, and hurriedly threw the covers off the bed. I had the horrible feeling that this unidentified crew member might be Mrs. Owada. I felt an inexplicable jolt of adrenaline run through my body.

I looked at Kyoko Hara's sleeping face, and saw that

she was breathing deeply, as people do when absolutely exhausted.

Two

The tall clock tower of the university loomed heavily against a gray sky. Remembering how many times I had visited the university with the white of the clock tower highlighted by a blue sky, I couldn't help feeling that this was a significant change in the weather.

Since my last visit, two of the people involved in the affair had already died. One was my patient, Akio Tanno, who had killed himself. Then there was Captain Owada's death in the crash. I felt a heavy responsibility for these two deaths. Perhaps I should have taken my patient's statement more seriously, or interpreted it more literally. Had I been too ready to conclude that he was simply deranged?

With a heavy heart, I knocked on the door of the professor's office in the department of European history. Professor Miyakawa had a book open in front of him at his desk, but on seeing my face he stood up rapidly, as if startled. His eyes hadn't been on the book from the beginning.

"I thought you'd probably come," he said. He tried to smile, but the twitching of his cheeks somehow spoiled the effect. I sat down opposite the professor without saying anything. As far as possible I wanted to allow him to speak first.

"You know the police came and asked me all sorts of questions about that student who killed himself," he began, "but I just told them I couldn't help. It seems he was being held under observation, but I really didn't know anything about it. You see, there are so many students in this place that it's all you can do to remember their faces. . . ."

He seemed to be searching for the right word, and stared blankly ahead of him. I let my gaze fall onto the book that the professor had in front of him. Comically, he was holding the book upside down. He was obviously extremely nervous, and unable to calm himself.

The professor noticed where I was looking, and hurriedly placed both hands on the book. "I'm reading about the fall of the Third Reich at the moment, you know. As the war came to an end, all the leading figures started dying off. . . ." The professor's words seemed strangely significant.

I opened my mouth to speak. "Do you know that Captain Owada died in an accident?" I asked.

"I did see it in the paper, but what does that have to do with anything?" asked the professor.

"Well, you see, the apartment where young Tanno caused all that trouble was in fact owned by Captain Owada."

"I see." The professor's face indicated surprise, but it was obviously a pretense.

"And do you also know that there was a third person on board the plane that crashed?" I asked.

"Yes, I do remember seeing something about it."

"And did you also see that they've discovered that

the unidentified body was a woman? I believe it was in the papers this morning . . ."

"No, I didn't see that," he said. "You see, I haven't been paying much attention to the local news section of the papers recently." The professor's cheeks were still twitching.

"I see. But people are talking about this all over town. You see, the autopsy showed that the woman had been dead for more than six months," I said.

"That's of no interest to me."

"Is that so? You see, it seems that she would have been about five foot two inches tall, and weighed about one hundred five pounds. Does that remind you of anyone you know?"

"What do you mean? There's no reason at all why I should know the woman. She's obviously a foreigner."

"The result of the autopsy shows that she was an Oriental," I said.

"In that case, she was probably Vietnamese."

I looked directly at the professor. "This morning I visited the town hall of a particular ward in Tokyo. It happens to be the ward where you reside."

The professor said nothing.

"You will probably think me impertinent, but I took the liberty of examining your family register. Your wife's maiden name appears to be Fumiko Hayashi. Furthermore, you divorced her a year ago, didn't you?"

"What's that got to do with anything? Why are you prying into my private life?" he spluttered. He seemed determined to resist to the end.

"And where is your ex-wife now?"

"There's no reason why I should tell you that."

"Do you remember when I asked you before whether you knew a woman named Fumiko? You showed me the register of all the students, I believe . . ."

"What you asked me, if I remember correctly, was whether there was a woman with that name among the students."

"That's correct, But you see, if you had told me then that your wife's name was also Fumiko . . ."

"What the hell are you talking about? Are you trying to threaten me? There's no reason why Akio Tanno should have known anything about my private life. There's absolutely no way . . ." The professor's whole body shook with rage. Whatever I said, he seemed determined not to face the facts.

"If it were to emerge that Akio Tanno had known your wife, would you cooperate with me?" I asked.

"Well, yes, I suppose that I would . . . but my ex-wife was certainly not five foot two, absolutely not, no way!" The professor hid his face in his book and began to sob.

"If you're not sure where your wife is now, I think you'd better get in touch with the police," I said quietly.

"But Fumiko is alive . . . Look, I don't want to get involved with this, it's so embarrassing," he mumbled. The professor was obviously beyond reasoning with. There wasn't any point in my continuing, since it wasn't really my business. I stood up and left the room.

I went straight over to a classroom in the music department. The choir was practicing Beethoven's Ninth for the New Year's concert. Michiko Hayashi came running out to meet me, her hair held as usual in a blue ribbon. She was carrying a stack of music in her arms.

"How nice to see you again, Doctor. You know, we held a collection for Akio Tanno's funeral, but we didn't know where to send it to. . . . Will he be buried in his hometown, do you think?"

"Yes, his remains have already been sent home." I looked at Michiko's innocent face.

"You know, in a strange way I actually feel relieved that Akio is dead," she said. "I can't really explain why I feel like that, but I just do." She probably felt a sense of satisfaction that her ideal love could now remain unsullied forever.

"Do you happen to know whether Akio ever visited Professor Miyakawa's home?" I asked her.

"Let me see . . . in our first year he did once say that he wanted to go over to the professor's house to talk about his tuition fees, but I don't know if anything came of it."

"Well, it doesn't really matter," I said. Now that I had asked her what I needed to know, I left the university through the front gate. I went into the café around the corner for a cup of coffee, only to find that the waitress with the sullen face still served the coffee with the same expression, and that the sausages were still rotating on the hot dog machine.

Three

A large metal grille had been installed over the pool outside Mrs. Owada's apartment house. But the stagnant water of the pool remained unchanged.

"I want to be the duckweed bobbing in a pool."

I spoke this line from Akio Tanno's poem aloud. Probably no one would ever go near the water of the pool again, I thought. I climbed the steps of the fire escape to Mrs. Owada's apartment on the sixth floor. If only the fire escape had been more visible from the front of the building, I couldn't help feeling, the whole thing would have ended up quite differently.

Were actions so easily affected by circumstances? I wondered. But again, this affair would probably have happened no matter where the fire escape had been. After all, there wasn't much you could do to change people's natures.

I found myself thinking about the old debate in Europe between nature and nurture, and the extent to which people are influenced by their environment. But it was really just a riddle, like the chicken and the egg. And the reason I was thinking of it in the first place was Mrs. Owada.

I knocked on the door of the apartment, which was draped in black mourning colors. After a while Mrs. Owada appeared, looking more beautiful than ever, almost like a classical eighteenth-century painting. She was wearing a delicate lace mourning dress over black satin.

"The door from the fire escape was open, so I came up that way. I really am most sorry . . . I don't know what to say. . . ." I said this awkwardly. It was now a week since Captain Owada's funeral, which had been held at the Aoyama cemetery.

"Yes, I left the door to the fire escape open myself," she said. "I somehow felt that if I left it open my husband might come home again."

She invited me through to the sunroom. The rubber plant and the other tropical plants were back where they had been before, but now the room was decorated in black and dark green.

"I've always done my best to avoid using black, but in the end here I am with it all around me," she said.

I tried to comfort her. "I hope you will soon be able to try a different color. Sadness is something that we should try to forget as soon as possible."

Mrs. Owada offered me a cup of tea, and as she did so I noticed that her hand was shaking slightly.

"I didn't expect you to say that to me," she said. "I was convinced you thought I had killed your patient. But I couldn't bring myself to let him have his way with me, no matter how hard I tried. I know that if I'd let him do it, he might not have killed himself, but I just couldn't stand the idea of it. My husband never seemed to have any difficulty in having other women. It seems a man can have many different loves. You see, he even had a woman with him when he died."

"But why do you think he had a woman with him?

Haven't you heard that they found out at the autopsy that the third person in the wreckage had died six months before?"

"No, that can't be. Everybody is just saying that to me so I won't be upset. But I'm sure that it was a girl-friend."

"But these days forensic science can determine the sex and even the time of death from charred bones," I said. I was trying to be as kind to her as possible. Mrs. Owada's shoulders drooped. She stood up and poured me another cup of tea. I changed the subject.

"You remember the dedication in that book of poems you gave me? You told me that Fumiko was your dead sister, didn't you."

"That's right."

"Is it possible that she was not your blood sister?" I asked.

"She was a sister in spirit." She said this without showing the slightest reaction. But I was sure that she knew perfectly well what we were talking about.

"I wonder if you would allow me to meet this spiritual sister of yours."

"I'm afraid that's really not possible." A slight smile played on her lips, and she placed one hand on her elegant bust.

"You see, this sister was simply a figment of my imagination. She never really existed, so there's no way that I can introduce you to her."

With this, she stood up. I thought it was a signal that I should go, but it wasn't. She went into her bedroom and removed her mourning clothes, reappearing with a large yellow and red bath towel wrapped around her.

"I've been waiting for someone I know well to come and visit, so that I can give the mourning a break and do some sunbathing . . . Even in winter, a touch of sun can help you forget the troubles of the world, you know, if only for a few moments."

She lay facedown on the couch. Her shapely legs and her well-formed buttocks were exposed to my view. The impression was all the stronger and fresher as she had just been wearing mourning clothes. I couldn't tear my eyes away from her. I felt a powerful desire for her.

"You know, I don't really believe my husband is dead," she said. "As soon as I heard of the accident I rushed over to the airport, but as I watched the burning aircraft, I decided to believe that my husband was not dead. After that I took a taxi and went over to the hotel."

I felt my face change color. I watched her closely to see what she was going to say.

"I took my usual room. My husband was making love to his young flight attendant in the next room . . . I thought to myself what a jealous wife I was. But I turned on the tape recorder anyway."

"And you heard the sounds of two people making love, I suppose?" I waited to hear what Mrs. Owada would say. So the night that Kyoko Hara and I had made love, she had been in the room next door. Was she trying to threaten me? Or did she merely think that I was the ghost of her dead husband?

I was unable to keep my silence. "That evening, the

person who was with Kyoko Hara was me. It wasn't your husband," I said.

"No, it was definitely my husband. He had just appeared in your form. If not, how could you do such a shameful thing? It's unthinkable."

She stood up and stretched out her hands toward me. The bath towel that had been wrapped around her fell to the floor. She was not wearing anything underneath. Her perfectly shaped breasts and marble-smooth skin shone in the sun. I couldn't decide how serious she was, but I knew that I would have to treat her with great care at this point. And the best way of doing this was to show her that I believed what she was doing. The last thing you should do is to damage a patient's self-esteem.

I stretched out my arms to touch her as she was obviously asking me to do, and our lips met. After a few moments she started loosening my tie, and began sighing deeply. I knew that if things continued like this, I would definitely be able to satisfy myself about one thing. And that was, whether or not Mrs. Owada was actually capable of loving a man. . . .

But when we finally lay naked together, she pushed me away from her as I had expected.

The Pool

One

It was the middle of the night. It must have been around two o'clock in the morning, and I was having a dream. The knock on my door somehow blended in with the sound of my own frantic screaming. I was standing in front of a dark hole. By the time I realized where I was, my body seemed to have already slipped halfway into a bottomless pit. I was desperately trying to claw my way out, and it was the sound of my own screaming which finally woke me up. I put on a robe and went to the door. I had no idea who could be visiting me at this time of night. But it was definitely a woman's voice I could hear, shouting as she banged on the door. I immediately thought of Motoko Kusano, head nurse at the hospital. Had she come bringing some urgent message?

I opened the door to see Fumiko Kawakami, her upper body swaying drunkenly as if she were about to fall over. I was quite sure that as usual she was stoned on a mixture of beer and sleeping pills. Whatever the reason, using sleeping pills so much at her age was a definite sign of instability. I held back the anger I could feel rising inside me, and reverted to the calm, professional attitude that I used for dealing with patients.

"What's the matter with you, so late at night . . . has something happened?" I asked.

"Please let me stay with you tonight, Doc. You see, I just feel so lonely . . . ," she said, in a pathetic voice.

"Well, all right then," I said. "But only if you promise to be quiet. The neighbors get very upset about noise."

I put some coffee on. She really looked in a state. She was wearing a cheap blouse and skirt of the sort you saw on sale in the teenage section of a department store, but her clothes were smeared with mud and food, and quite filthy.

"How on earth did you find out where I live?" I asked.

"I called up the hospital and told them that I was contacting old classmates for a school reunion, so they gave me your address," she said, with a cheeky grin.

"I'm amazed how you can do it when you have to, though you're obviously out of it on sleeping pills most of the time."

"I don't really understand it myself . . . but sometimes I get these moments when I see things very clearly. You know, it even scares me. You see, this evening I suddenly felt really afraid."

"You've just realized something, haven't you?" I said.

I smiled at her gently, as if talking to a patient, trying to show that I understood. But she wouldn't look at me. Then suddenly she started to take off the clothes she was wearing.

"You know Doc, I'm really cold. Do you mind if I take a bath?"

"If you must . . . but please keep the noise down," I said. "I don't want the neighbors coming over." I felt I had to do what I could to make her feel comfortable. I was sure she had something very important to tell me about Akio Tanno. She seemed to be pleased that I was being nice to her, sticking out her tongue and laughing at me as she skipped to the bathroom.

She was in the bathroom so long that I began to get worried. I had heard her running the water at first, but when that stopped I didn't hear a sound for more than ten minutes. I was getting very nervous. There was an old-style open razor in front of the bathroom mirror. With a thing like that she could easily cut her jugular. I suddenly realized how stupid I'd been to let her go in so easily like that without thinking like a doctor.

I knocked on the bathroom door, but there was no reply. I was quite prepared to break the glass to get in if she'd locked herself in, but when I turned the handle the door opened easily enough. She was fast asleep on the tiled floor, her pert little breasts pointing upward and her legs spread wide apart. Apart from the lather from the soap she had used, she was completely naked. With her clothes on she looked very adult at times, but to see her like this it was obvious how young she was. Her body looked just like an unripe fruit.

I shook her gently. I decided it would be best for me to act in my professional capacity as a doctor from the start. That way, there would be no need for me to avert my eyes. Just as you would with a child, I wiped her down with a towel and carried her over to my bed. In the process, however, I noticed that she had countless red marks on her shoulders and arms, and even inside her thighs. They were quite clearly teeth marks.

I started to get angry again. Why did she have to go on hurting herself like this? And how had she managed to do this to herself, anyway? Was it at one of those Harajuku parties? But at the parties people always kept at least some of their clothes on. The unspoken rule was not to take all your clothes off. Had she taken some more pills and gone off with a rich pervert? I'd seen some money stuffed casually into her coat pocket earlier.

Feeling something close to despair, I pulled the blanket up to her chin and left her to sleep. But suddenly she opened her eyes and stretched out her arms toward me.

"Know what, Doc? I've just found myself a real nice sugar daddy," she said mischievously.

"If that's really true, you shouldn't be feeling lonely, should you? Why did you come over like this to my place?"

"I don't really know. But you see, it started to get a bit weird, so in the end I bit back." She gave a quick laugh, and laying her head back on the pillow suddenly dropped off into a deep sleep again. I went over to my liquor cabinet, had a slug of brandy, and settled down on the couch.

When I woke up in the morning, she was gone. The blanket was folded neatly on the bed, and on the side table, folded neatly in a lace handkerchief, I found a rifle shell. Next to it was a neatly written note in her handwriting.

"This is what Akio Tanno killed Mrs. Owada with."

Since Mrs. Owada was obviously still alive, there was something odd about the note she'd written. I decided to take the shell with me to the forensic department at the university and have it analyzed.

But when I went back to get the results, the assistant gave me a suspicious look, and told me it was the case for a blank.

Two

The rented car I was driving spun its rear wheels slightly as I took a sharp curve in the mountain road. There was already some black ice forming on the asphalt.

"Are we going to make it?" In the passenger seat, Kyoko Hara moved toward me with a worried look. She was wearing a fur coat that Captain Owada had bought for her in Spain. She was still mourning deeply for him.

"It's much colder up here than on the plain, you know. It could be almost ten degrees below by the time we get to Professor Miyakawa's cabin," I said.

"Do we really have to go and meet Professor Miyakawa?" she asked me again. "Now that Captain Owada is dead, I'd really rather prefer to leave everything the way it is."

I felt the same way myself. But in point of fact, nothing had really been resolved. I'd decided I would have to see the professor once again and get him to talk. This time I wanted the truth. Just as a fruit ripens and eventually drops, there comes a time when a person is ready to talk.

Arriving at the professor's cabin, I knew that I'd been right to come. The professor was standing in front of a brightly burning charcoal brazier, burning a bundle of letters.

"I thought you might find your way up here," he said. "I'm just burning this pile of old letters from my wife. Before we got married, we used to write a lot of letters to one another, you know." The professor looked genuinely upset. It was hard to believe that he could be just acting. When I introduced Kyoko Hara to him as Captain Owada's girlfriend, the professor shot a brief glance in her direction and nodded slowly.

"Captain Owada told her all about the situation," I said. "Before he took off for his final flight, it seems he told her everything he knew."

"So he told her about my wife, then?" The professor seemed to have been expecting it.

"Yes, he did," I said, nodding. The professor bowed his head and started to talk, almost as if he was relieved. He'd obviously been looking for an opportunity to make a confession. He'd clearly given up any hope of fobbing me off with lies. Kyoko moved slightly away from us and sat down on the sofa. I thought that it would be better for her, too, to know the truth. It would make it easier for her to pick up the pieces and start life again.

"The first time Akio Tanno came to my house was some eight months ago." The professor looked across to the wall of his cabin, which was like a sort of Finnish log hut. On the wall was a calendar and a glass case for a hunting rifle, fitted with a strong lock. The case was empty.

"He'd come to see me about his tuition fees, but I wasn't in. My wife felt sorry for him, and lent him enough money for the next term. It seems he mistakenly thought she'd done this for him out of love, and so on a number of occasions after that he came up to visit my wife when he knew I was out. As you are no doubt aware, we didn't have any children. In time, Fumiko came to love him herself. You see, it's painful for me to have to say this, but for several years prior to that we had been married in name only. I had even become impotent for a time . . ."

The professor turned his back to us and started raking over the charcoal in the brazier. Just like a patient who has come for psychoanalysis, there were lies mixed in with the truth. As he started his confession, the professor was unconsciously testing my resistance to these lies. But a good part of what he was saying was true, and given the opportunity, he could still be steered back in the direction of the truth.

I held out Mrs. Owada's book of poems to him. "Have you ever seen this anthology?" I asked.

"No," he said, shaking his head. I opened her book, *The White Summer,* to the page with its dedication "To Fumiko," and held it up for him to see.

"This is a dedication from Mrs. Owada to your wife. When did your wife first start visiting Mrs. Owada at her apartment?"

"It must have been when she joined the poetry group." The professor stood up again somewhat unsteadily, and sat down heavily in an armchair in front of the fire. He stared vacantly in the direction of the brazier.

"Could you tell us something about the relationship between your wife and Mrs. Owada?" I asked.

"I suppose that they loved one another . . . You see, my wife is the type who constantly wants other people to tell her how beautiful she is. Mrs. Owada seemed keen to get to know her, and after a while I think their relationship became physical. In other words, the two of them were lesbians. . . . She took to leaving our house in the daytime and going over to visit Mrs. Owada in her apartment."

"And what happened to her relationship with Akio Tanno?"

"I suspect she gradually turned him away. I'm really not very sure, you see . . . but coincidence is a very frightening thing, you know. My wife had been trying to avoid him, but one day when she was at Mrs. Owada's, Akio Tanno turned up with a delivery from the department store where he was working part-time as a delivery boy. My wife went to the door to take it instead of Mrs. Owada. They must have been really surprised to see each other. My wife asked him to come into the room. She wanted her lover Mrs. Owada to see her embracing a young man. You see she was . . . she was that sort of woman. She liked to do provocative things." The professor suddenly stood up and began waving his arms around in excitement.

"Akio Tanno began to plot his revenge on my wife, who he felt had betrayed him. He said to me one day that he wanted to borrow my hunting rifle. So he took the rifle that was in that case."

"And then what happened?"

"I honestly don't know . . . it's true . . . I think that, as he said himself, he killed her with the gun. I haven't had a good night's sleep since my wife stopped coming home. I was terrified that the body would turn up somehow . . . it obsessed me. You see if it ever came to light, the scandal would ruin me."

"But they finally found her, didn't they," I said. "By a lucky chance they managed to identify her from the charred remains discovered in the wreckage of that jet that crashed the other day."

I wanted to push on to the end. The evening air high up in the mountains around the cabin was quiet and still, but occasionally a freezing wind rustled the leaves of the trees outside.

"That may be so . . . ," said the professor, "but fortunately her body was completely burnt up. All I want to do now is to forget this whole nightmare. Both my wife and her murderer are dead and buried. It was a military aircraft that crashed, so it's not a matter for criminal investigation. The Japanese police will not be able to investigate. And as for you, I am talking to you as a doctor. I expect you to respect my privacy." The professor squatted down again in front of the fire. It seemed it was now my turn to speak.

"You say that the first time Akio Tanno came to your house, he came of his own accord. But in actual fact, isn't it the truth that you told him he should come over to your house to discuss the fees if he was worried about them?" I asked.

The professor's shoulders started to shake.

"He wasn't the first student you had asked over to your house, was he?" I continued. "There must have been plenty of other young men who came. Most of them were handsome boys with fit young bodies like Akio. All of them got special attention and love from your wife. Innocent young men coming up to the university from a country town were bound to be lonely in their unfamiliar new lives, and quite literally starving for love. In most cases your wife was probably their first guide into the new world of sex. All of them were in their most vulnerable years, both physically and mentally, and were easily driven to feelings of guilt through their relations with the wife of their professor."

"It's a lie, that's pure fantasy on your part . . . It's quite preposterous," spluttered the professor.

Ignoring his protest, I carried on. "You always waited until the time was right and then called the students to your office. You threatened them, saying your wife had confessed everything to you. Then you asked them what they were going to do about it. As their professor and your wife's husband, you put them in an impossible position. And then you gave them the terms on which they could escape from their dilemma."

"You're lying!" he cried.

"You made them have sex with you. The only reason you married a beautiful wife in the first place was to create an excuse to lure young men into your life."

The professor fell silent. But I could see that his shoulders were heaving. I pressed on. "That gun case is not broken, is it? Akio Tanno did not take that gun. You gave it to him, didn't you?"

"No, you're wrong there, you really are . . . the gun just disappeared one day. If he says he used it to shoot someone then he must have taken it himself. You must believe me, please."

"If you will acknowledge that what I've been saying is true, then I'll believe you. I just want to know the truth."

"I'm prepared to acknowledge it, but I didn't plan it as you suggest. It just happened that way. It's true that men excite me. But surely . . . that's my own private business." It was obviously difficult for the professor to get these words out. Holding his face in both hands, he rolled over onto the floor.

I took the pale-looking Kyoko Hara by the hand and led her outside. I felt no hatred for the professor. I just felt that he shouldn't be working as a teacher. To abuse one's position in that way and to harm innocent young men was unforgivable.

"Captain Owada really got himself into trouble, didn't he?" said Kyoko. "I only wish that he'd been able to tell me about it . . ."

"He probably thought nobody would understand him," I said.

"Do you think everything Professor Miyakawa has just told us is true?" she asked.

"No, not completely. But I think we've got all we can from him at this stage. The most important thing now is whether Mrs. Owada will tell her side of the story."

"That's going to be difficult," she said. "It will be hard for you to talk to her as you did to the professor, because you're in love with her yourself."

I said nothing and put the car in gear. In the hour that we had been there, the windshield had turned white with frost.

Three

A few days later I found myself once again climbing the fire escape at Leila Mansions. It was just after ten o'clock in the morning, and the thin rays of the winter sun lit up the east side of the building. Mrs. Owada would be doing her morning sunbathing. I was sure that her current mental state was probably quite finely balanced between reality and illusion. It would be up to her to decide which way to go forward. I hoped very much that she would choose the world of reality.

When she opened the door, Mrs. Owada was wearing

her usual black lace mourning dress. Although she had toned it down, she was nonetheless wearing makeup. She looked as though she had been waiting for me to call. "You must be tired, my dear," she said. "Who was your copilot today?" She took off my jacket and brought over Captain Owada's dressing gown for me. The sleeves of the brown dressing gown were embroidered with dragons. Mrs. Owada ran her slim fingers over the embroidery and pressed her cheek against mine.

"I'm so lonely when you're away, you know," she said.

"I suppose you've been doing your sunbathing, again?" I asked.

"Yes, I put in an hour this morning."

"And did Fumiko come over today?"

"Fumiko . . . ? Oh yes, she was here." Mrs. Owada's eyes had a glazed look about them.

I went on playing the role of her husband, as she obviously wanted me to. I was sure that the two of them would have discussed Fumiko many times.

My eye was suddenly caught by the enormous white door of the refrigerator in her kitchen. It was far too big for her tiny apartment. It was a large American model of the type used in restaurants. The freezer compartment would be way below zero . . . I wondered what had made her buy such a large new refrigerator. Then I suddenly remembered how her sunbathing couch had been wet one day when I came. At the time I was sure it was because she had just taken a shower.

But was that the real reason? I began to feel a shiver rising up my spine.

"Did you have a good chat with Fumiko when she came?" I asked.

"Yes, thank you."

"Did you sunbathe together with her as usual?"

"No, we didn't today," she said, "You see, she's very sensitive to the cold." Mrs. Owada still had her cheek pressed up against mine. The mourning dress she had on today had long sleeves and was tight at the neck, and she looked the very picture of a respectable widow, with all her beautiful skin covered up.

"I'd like you to try and remember the time when Fumiko died. Akio Tanno brought up a hunting rifle hidden in a box, didn't he?" I said, putting my arm around her shoulders and drawing her toward me. But as I did so she suddenly stood up and pushed against me with all her strength. Then she abruptly went over and stood by the window, turning her back to me.

"Let's give up this charade, shall we?" she said. "Perhaps you think it's amusing, but I certainly don't. You don't understand anything about the world of dreams, do you? You're the sort of person who won't rest until he measures everything in terms of facts."

"But that's because it is a fact that someone has died. It's only natural that people should be suspicious. You have to be able to explain it."

"You can explain it as much as you like. As you have already guessed, Akio Tanno did indeed meet Fumiko here. You see, after the divorce from her husband, I had her working here for a while as a housekeeper when my husband was away. But although I would normally answer the door myself, on the day that Akio came with his delivery I was doing some washing, so Fumiko went. But there's no point in regretting that now. Anyhow, after that Akio kept phoning and asking to meet Fumiko. I refused. You see I'd made a pact with Fumiko to die together . . . We were in love, you see. But of course it was merely platonic."

"Was she such a wonderful woman, then?" I asked.

In answer to my question, Mrs. Owada took out a photograph album and brought it over to me. There was a picture of Fumiko Miyakawa at a time when, for a brief moment, she was being heralded as a new star of the stage. It showed her in the role of Helen of Troy, with a broad grin on her face. I didn't think she was particularly beautiful myself, but there was no doubt she had something that would appeal quite strongly to a certain type of person.

"An elegant woman, wasn't she?" I said.

I handed the album back to Mrs. Owada. She held the photo of Fumiko against herself as if cradling a child.

"Fumiko herself wanted to die. She was the one who brought the hunting rifle from her husband's lodge. You see, we had this plan to shoot ourselves in a double suicide, the sort of thing young boys think about. Fumiko pulled the trigger first."

After a short pause, she continued her story. "But just as she did so the door of the apartment opened and somebody came in. I was scared, and hid behind a curtain."

"It was Akio Tanno, wasn't it?" I said.

"Yes, it was. He'd had a key made and let himself in. He thought it was just Fumiko who lived in this apartment. You see, to try to get rid of him, Fumiko had once told him that she'd married a man called Owada after her divorce from her husband. And Akio really believed it. To be able to meet her, he pressed some wax into the lock from outside and made himself a key. So all those things he said in his statement about bringing a box over to get the door opened, he just made all that up. But when he came into the room and saw that Fumiko was dead, he screamed. He was convinced that she'd killed herself because he'd been bothering her so much. You see, he'd been threatening to tell her new husband everything that had happened between them. That's why he insisted to you that he'd killed Mrs. Owada."

"But why was the chain not on when he opened the door with the key he had made?" I asked.

"I'd taken it off because I thought my husband wouldn't be able to get in after we'd killed ourselves," she said.

Her explanation was at least logical, but I still didn't believe everything that she said. It reminded me of a novel by Akutagawa which I'd read as a young student. The story is about three people involved in a crime who all give completely different versions of what happened, so that in the end you're left with no idea of what the truth was. But who was lying here?

Just at that moment the sunlight coming through the window lit up the lace on Mrs. Owada's shoulder.

Through the semitransparent material I could see what looked like bruises on her skin. I went closer to her, and after first kissing her on the cheek, roughly pulled down the shoulder of her mourning dress. The bruises were teeth marks.

A few days before, when Fumiko Kawakami had come to my apartment in the middle of the night, she'd told me that she'd bitten someone. I remembered it very clearly. Could it be that the "sugar daddy" she talked about was in fact Mrs. Owada? But if so, why had she given Fumiko money? Perhaps when Fumiko was stoned she'd remembered something important about Akio Tanno. Mrs. Owada would have wanted to keep her quiet.

I started to feel a chill running up my spine. Almost without thinking, I found my gaze resting on the large refrigerator in the kitchen. Mrs. Owada put her arm around my shoulder and snuggled up to kiss me. Then she noticed where I was looking, and without changing her expression casually pulled down the window blind with her free hand.

A shadow fell across our faces.

A Cracked Bottom

One

The surface of the pool was covered in green duckweed. Bits of dry wood and leaves were floating in clumps on the surface, as if some kids had thrown them in. But the level of the water in the pool was visibly dropping as I watched. A large red fire engine was parked at the side of the pool and was pumping the water out.

"I wonder what we're going to find. Do you suppose it could possibly be another body?" The police superintendent came over to where I was standing and asked me this with something approaching relish.

The call had come through from the forensic department, so the superintendent himself had come over specially to supervise the operation. I had the feeling that we were now near the end of the trail. I felt rather like a child at the end of an absorbing film, rather sad to see it all drawing to a close.

"I don't know what might turn up. I suppose it could well be another body," I said.

"I hope the information is reliable," said the superintendent. "We've gone to all this trouble to bring a fire engine along. It'll look pretty silly if we don't find anything. Still, it won't be altogether a bad thing if we don't find a body, I suppose . . ."

He said this as a joke, but there was an intent expression on his face as he watched the steadily draining pool. By now more than half of the water was gone. If there was a body in there, we should have been able to see it by now. I felt a strange mixture of relief and anxiety. If nothing was found in the pool, I would have put them to all this trouble for nothing.

The water was now rapidly disappearing, and the bottom of the pool was nearly visible. The rubbish that had been floating on the surface was scattered around on the bottom. Just at that moment there was a shout from one of the work crew, who was wearing long wading boots. He'd seen something, a long object covered in weeds at the far end of the pool by the sluice.

"It's a rifle! There's a gun down there!"

"Go and get it, but be careful," barked the superintendent.

"Is that the rifle you've been looking for?" he asked me.

"I think so," I said.

I felt a pleasant sensation of relief. In all honesty I'd been worried that we would find the body of Fumiko Kawakami at the bottom of the pool, heavily weighted.

"Do you remember all that trouble there was with a university student who claimed he'd forced his way into an apartment on the sixth floor of this building and killed someone?" I asked the superintendent. "He was held under observation at my hospital, you know . . ."

"Oh, you mean the student who drowned himself in this pool a few months back," said the superintendent.

"That's right. I think that must be the rifle that he threw away in the pool."

"Well, when we found him we did drag the bottom of the pool . . . But I suppose we should have been more thorough." The superintendent looked disappointed. The pool's drainage system was broken and for the past year the pool had been kept as a water reserve for the fire brigade.

He went off to take charge of the rifle, and I went up to the sixth floor of Leila Mansions.

When I pressed the bell, Mrs. Owada came to the door immediately and invited me into the sunroom. She was still wearing her black lace mourning clothes.

"They've found the gun Akio Tanno described in his statement at the bottom of the pool," I said.

"Yes, I've been watching them from up here," she replied.

"Last time I was here you told me that Mrs. Miyakawa committed suicide. That she shot herself with the rifle . . . So was it you, then, who threw the rifle into the pool?" I asked.

She made no reply. As we entered the sunroom, I too fell silent, and stared blankly at the leaves of the green rubber plant. I suddenly got the feeling that Mrs.

Owada might be about to confess that in fact she'd shot Mrs. Miyakawa.

"I thought Akio had safely gotten rid of the gun somewhere. If it hadn't been found, then there'd be no need to do any more injury, either to his memory or to the other people still alive who know the real truth of this whole affair. As long as everyone still believed Fumiko had committed suicide, there was no need for it to get any further out of hand." She spoke briskly, in a businesslike fashion.

"Are you saying, then, that Akio Tanno did in fact kill Mrs. Miyakawa with the hunting rifle?"

"Well, I don't myself know whether it could strictly be said that he did kill her. But it's nonetheless a fact that he pointed the gun at her and pulled the trigger."

"And it's also a fact that the hunting rifle was brought to this room by Akio Tanno himself, isn't it?"

"That's right; he put it in a delivery box and brought it here. But it isn't quite as simple as all that."

Mrs. Owada heaved a sigh and lit the cigarette in her long cigarette holder.

"I suppose you are aware how Fumiko was treated after her marriage to the professor?" she asked.

"Yes, it's a most unpleasant story. I gather that Professor Miyakawa used her as a bait to lure young male students to his home."

"You see, she really just couldn't stand it. At first she thought she could get along with the idea that at least she was the wife of a university professor, with all the social standing that brings. But that illusion didn't last very long. She and I had been friends ever since we met by chance at a poetry circle, but one day she broke down and told me how much she was suffering. After her divorce, she left home and came to live here. The professor got to know where she was staying, but at first he pretended he didn't know. After a while he took it into his head to get her to come back. But out of the blue one day, young Akio, who was working part-time as a delivery boy, came to my apartment with a delivery. As it happened, Fumiko went to the door instead of me. They were both very surprised to see each other. You see, Akio had been in love with Fumiko. But Fumiko felt that she didn't want to be involved with him anymore, so she lied to him, saying that she was no longer Professor Miyakawa's wife, but had married again and was now Mrs. Owada. Of course young Akio took her at her word, and that was the start of this terrible story."

In marked contrast to the previous times she'd spoken about it, this time Mrs. Owada told her story unhesitatingly. She had clearly lost the will to go on with the deception. It seemed as if she'd come to the conclusion that there was no longer anybody to hide the truth for. I turned away from her, and looked down at the pool below. It was now quite empty of water. The "Members Only" sign lay where it had been pushed to one side, under the row of cypress trees.

Two

"Please tell me more about the day of the murder. I'm talking about the day that Akio Tanno killed Mrs. Miyakawa."

"On the day before Akio arrived, Professor Miyakawa telephoned me here at the apartment. He told me that Akio Tanno was on his way here with a hunting rifle. He said that Akio seemed to be intent on killing Fumiko, as he now believed that Fumiko had become Mrs. Owada. He wanted me to take her away from the apartment, warning me that Akio was likely to bring the gun in a box wrapped in paper from the department store. You see, Akio had told the professor that Fumiko was here."

"But despite his warning, you let him in, did you?" I asked.

"Well you see, Professor Miyakawa told me that he'd lent young Akio his gun but that he'd replaced the bullets with blanks, so that if it went off it would simply make a noise. He said that Akio had gotten obsessed about the whole thing, and that no matter what anyone said to him he wouldn't understand. He said that he was a young man who couldn't be reasoned with until he did something, so it was best to let him have his way. But to allow him to do this without causing any real damage, we would have to plan it very carefully in advance."

"So you decided to have a little drama, then, did you?"

"That's right. When I told her what her husband had said, Fumiko agreed to go through with it. After we had let him fire the blank, she said that we should make it look as if she were bleeding to death and really ham it up. She was quite taken with the idea."

Perhaps the idea of pretending to be dead and giving a young boy a shock appealed to Fumiko, who at one time had been a hopeful young actress. I now began to understand how the four of them had gotten involved in this sorry business.

"Pretending to be making a delivery from the department store, Akio Tanno came up the fire escape at two o'clock in the afternoon. Fumiko took the chain off the door and started to let him in. As she stepped back into the apartment, Akio took the hunting rifle out of the delivery box and pulled the trigger. After the gun went off, I could hear his voice echoing right through to the bathroom where I was hiding, screaming at her, 'You betrayed me, I was so in love with you . . . You've ruined my life!' I felt so sorry for him after that. When you really fall in love, it's not surprising if you get carried away. I heard Akio leaving the apartment, so I came out into the bedroom. I was about to say to her that there was no need to get so carried away with the amateur dramatics. But when I looked down at her I saw that she really had been shot, right through the heart, and that she was quite dead."

"And did Akio Tanno take the gun that he used to shoot her with him when he left?"

"He did. It wasn't in the room after he'd gone."

I wondered why Akio Tanno had forgotten that he'd

thrown the hunting rifle into the swimming pool. The only explanation could be that in his excited state after the murder he'd had a temporary attack of amnesia.

"But why didn't you call the police and ambulance right away?"

"I was too confused. I couldn't understand why there had been a real bullet in the gun. I put in a call to the professor at the university, but was told that he was lecturing and wouldn't be available for another two hours. For two hours I sat next to Fumiko's dead body. I was so sad and shocked that I just didn't know what to do. But while I was sitting there my husband came home. As soon as he saw her lying there dead, he was convinced that I'd shot her."

"Did you explain to him that Akio Tanno had done it?"

"Yes, of course I did, and my husband said that he understood, but I know that in fact he didn't believe me. You see, he was convinced that Fumiko and I were lovers."

"And were you in fact lovers?" I asked.

"Well, if we were, it was only at a platonic level. It seems that my husband suspected that we were more deeply involved. You see, my husband, like most ordinary people, thought that there must be something very strange going on."

"And what did your husband do then?"

"That evening he went over to see an American friend of his and borrowed a large refrigerator of the type they use in restaurants, one that could be used for deep-freeze storage. You see an apartment is different from an ordinary house; there isn't anywhere where you can just go out and bury a body. My husband's only concern seemed to be how to dispose of Fumiko's body. You must remember that he believed I'd shot Fumiko. He was convinced that it was his responsibility to save me from being arrested by the police. He wanted to prove to himself by doing this that he loved me, or at the very least that he was able to protect me."

"Well, I must admit that I too thought that you had killed Mrs. Miyakawa."

"And do you still think so now?" She asked me this in her usual quiet voice. She looked directly at me with a glance that betrayed no emotion. But before I could answer her, she went on.

"The police finally arrived two days later. It was two days after the event that Akio finally went to the police and confessed that he'd killed Mrs. Owada. But when the police came they were able to confirm that I was still alive, so there was nothing they could do. If only he had said that he'd killed a woman, it would have been different. But he kept insisting that he'd killed Mrs. Owada. On top of that, he had no weapon to show them which could have been used as the murder weapon."

I now began to understand the psychological process whereby Akio Tanno, feeling that nobody would listen to what he was saying, had started to feel that, after all, he must be crazy.

"My husband seemed to think that I must be some kind of sick lesbian. In that sense I think he really thought I was mentally ill. He began to think that it was his duty to dispose of the body for the sake of his disturbed wife. So when his company started taking on military flights to Vietnam, and didn't have enough staff to handle it, my husband put in for a transfer. Military aircraft aren't subject to customs checks, and don't leave at scheduled times. When he heard that there was a special flight coming in, my husband took a military cart that he'd put aside for the purpose, and loaded the wooden box containing Fumiko's frozen body onto the airplane. He told me to write a poem because he was going to bury her at sea, in the deep blue sea. I pretended to be mad, and wrote some poems for Fumiko."

"I'm amazed that you were able to carry on your everyday life with a dead body in your freezer," I said.

"There were times when I started to feel afraid that perhaps I really was crazy after all. You see I had to pretend that I was sunbathing with Fumiko every day. My husband felt relieved when the couch in the sunroom was wet."

"But why did you have to keep up this self-destructive game for so long?" I asked.

"Well you see, whatever form it had to take, I wanted to preserve some semblance of love between myself and my husband."

"But you knew that your husband was having an affair with a young flight attendant, didn't you?"

"Yes, and that's why I resisted him. You see, I'm fastidious to an almost unhealthy degree. But now I feel it wasn't right to have involved a young person in a marital problem. Perhaps I should have told the police right away."

"And what did Professor Miyakawa say about the bullet in the hunting rifle?"

"He said he knew nothing about it. He said that Akio must have noticed that it was loaded with a blank and changed it for a real bullet. I know it may sound like an excuse, but I wanted to save that poor young boy from a murder charge. If there had been no other way of doing it, I was quite prepared to live with Fumiko's body forever."

Mrs. Owada looked directly into my eyes. I had finally come around to believing that what she was telling me was true. Perhaps it was because of my own secret love for her. I could see now that both her actions and her husband's sprang from the difficulty of their relationship. The actions of an incredibly selfish love . . .

"Well, the rifle has now been found, and a third body was discovered in the wreckage of your husband's plane, so I'm afraid it's not going to be possible for you to keep covering up what has happened. I think sooner or later you're going to have to go to the police."

"Yes, I know. If you wouldn't mind, could I ask you to go with me to the police station and help explain what has happened?"

"Before we do that, I have one more question I would like you to answer. Have you given any money recently to a young girl called Fumiko Kawakami?"

"No, not at all. When she came up to this room, she blurted out all of a sudden that she was sure that Fumiko was still alive after Akio had pulled the trigger. Then, she accused me of having killed Fumiko afterwards. When I didn't answer her she suddenly bit my shoulder, apologized, and then ran off. I have absolutely no idea why she did it."

For the first time I understood what it was that Fumiko Kawakami had been trying to do.

Three

When I arrived at Professor Miyakawa's cabin in Karuizawa, it was already too late. The freezing conditions in the mountain valleys had meant that I'd had to stop to put snow chains on my tires, which had taken even more time.

When I pushed open the door of the cabin, which had all its lights on, Professor Miyakawa was slumped in front of the fire. Next to him, holding a hunting rifle, was Fumiko Kawakami. She was staring ahead of her with a glazed look in her eye. I stretched out my hand, and she handed over the gun without protest.

"I killed him, you know. It was in revenge for Akio."

"But . . . he committed suicide, didn't he?" I asked.

"That's right, he did. But you see, before he died he remembered everything that had happened. At one point he had lost all confidence in himself. But before he died it all came back to him."

"But why have you killed Professor Miyakawa?"

"Because he was the one who lent a rifle to Akio. And I heard all about everything he did to Akio from Akio himself . . ."

"But I . . ." I stopped myself from going on. I didn't really know what to say. It seemed to me that because we'd interpreted Akio Tanno's statement in psychological terms, a murder had occurred that needn't have happened. I felt a heavy weight of responsibility fall onto my shoulders.

"When you came and stayed at my room the other day, I saw the injuries you had. What on earth happened to you?" I tried to keep up the appearance of being calm as I asked her this question.

"Oh, that. . . ." She glanced over in the direction of the man lying dead on the floor.

"He was the one who did that to me. He wanted me to go to the police and tell them that Mrs. Owada had done it. He wanted me to say that Mrs. Owada had been the one who killed Fumiko, that she'd killed her after Akio had fired the blank. He gave me some money, so at first I was going to do what he said, but on the way I changed my mind. You see, it was he who lent Akio Tanno the gun. The night Akio came back after killing the woman, I was with him the whole time. I was pretty far gone with the sleeping pills and everything, but I remember what he told me, though he was crying all the time. It finally came back to me two or three days ago. Everything he told me. The hunting rifle had a blank in it, and he told me that he took it out and replaced it with a real bullet. He said that the adults were all lying to him, trying to deceive him, but he wasn't going to be taken in. And then, you see, he gave me the shell. Take it as a keepsake, he said . . . I put it in my purse and it just stayed there at the bottom. That's why I know it wasn't Mrs. Owada who killed her."

"But the other evening you brought that shell over to my place, didn't you?" I said.

"That's right. I handed it over to you because I thought it was better for you to have it than me." Fumiko seemed not to be aware of the gravity of what she was saying. Feeling the weight of the moment upon me, I stared at the body lying on the floor at my feet. He didn't have to have died in this way.

I put my coat around her cold-looking shoulders, and led her out and into the backseat of my car. There was no phone for me to call the local police. Mrs. Owada, whom I had brought with me, was sitting in the passenger seat with her eyes shut.

"I'm being given the runaround by my patients right to the very end. Everybody has their own version of the truth. So there's nothing to do but believe your own truth," I said, but Mrs. Owada made no reply.

The car made its way down the mountain road, the chains clanking slowly on the snow.

"I want you to tell me one thing, though. Who is the person you love the most?" I asked.

"Why my husband, of course . . . Even now, he is the only one I love."

"If he hadn't died in that accident, would you have gone on with your marriage to him, without any changes?"

"I certainly could have. It's better than cutting off your feelings . . . But I'm sure you can't really understand how I feel," she said.

The car arrived in front of the police station. There was a police car parked in front of the entrance, with a layer of snow on its roof. I switched off the engine and looked into the backseat. There were small beads of sweat on Fumiko Kawakami's brow as she slept with an innocent-looking expression on her face.

"Even so, I didn't want to see young people getting involved like this, you know," I said.

Mrs. Owada looked down at Fumiko Kawakami's face for some time, but said nothing. I opened the car door and made my way up the gray steps of the police station to give my statement to the police. I suddenly felt much older. The thermometer on the wall stood at seventeen degrees below zero, and my breath froze white in the chill air.

About the Author

A well-known Japanese essayist, social commentator, and television personality, Masako Togawa is the author of over twenty books, three of which have been translated into English. Her first novel, *Oi Naru Genei (The Master Key)*, was awarded the prestigious Edogawa Ranpo Prize, while her second novel, *Ryojin Nikki (The Lady Killer)*, was adapted for film and Japanese television. She lives in Tokyo.

About the Translator

Simon Prentis spent eight years in Japan working as a translator and interpreter. He now lives in London, where he heads Simon Prentis Associates, an organization specializing in media projects involving Japan.